HONOR

Drakyn's Lady

K. M. Kirk

Eloquent Books

Copyright © 2010
All rights reserved – Kathleen M. Kirk

No part of this book may be reproduced or transmitted in any form or by any means, graphic, electronic, or mechanical, including photocopying, recording, taping, or by any information storage retrieval system, without the permission, in writing, from the publisher.

Eloquent Books
An imprint of Strategic Book Group
P.O. Box 333
Durham CT 06422
www.StrategicBookGroup.com

ISBN: 978-1-60911-524-1

Printed in the United States of America

Book Design: Rolando F. Santos

Contents

Chapter 1: Jeopardy 1

Chapter 2: Drakyn's Compulsion 15

Chapter 3: Awakening 27

Chapter 4: Anything.. 31

Chapter 5: Drakyn's Lady 35

Chapter 6: Unfettered 51

Chapter 7: Loss 63

Chapter 8: Discovery 77

Chapter 9: The Crew 93

Chapter 10: A Visitor 101

Chapter 11: Separation 109

Chapter 12: Piercing Space 117

Chapter 13: Insanity 123

Chapter 14: Bloody Vessel 135

Chapter 15: Deception 141

Chapter 16: Fools 145

Chapter 17: Sabotage 155

Chapter 18: Destruction 165

Chapter 19: Rescue 175

Chapter 20: Acceptance 183

Chapter 21: Everything.. 187

FOR my late father, *Michael F. Kirk*, who pointed out the stars to me as a child and told me about the many worlds we have yet to discover.

Also, I want to acknowledge my wonderful friends, Ann, Milena, Chris, JoAnn, Suzanne, and Sasha, who have encouraged me for years, helped me proofread, and have been great cheerleaders! Thanks, everyone!

Chapter 1

Jeopardy

THE crash killed me.

That's the shortest version of what happened to me on planet Viste. Of course, such a statement reveals nothing of what really occurred there. My death was the beginning of a new life—a life of a kind I had never even imagined. How strange that statement must seem, yet as I reflect upon all that came before and all that came following my human life, I am certain it is quite true.

Please note that I stress the word *human* before the word *life*. Everything changed that day on Viste—nothing was ever the same, and yet the possibilities have become almost limitless.

To understand my story, I must begin half a galaxy away from Viste. My partner, Koji Noguchi, and I had just completed our Planetary Fleet duty of more than ten solar months along the outermost border of Free Space, and we had been granted holiday time before we were expected back on Earth to accept new orders. Unlike most of the rest of the crew, Koji and I had interests other than home and family; we worked together on refining the details of the ship we had designed and then built as ensigns in the Academy. Now, we retrieved our prototype ship from Star Base 7 and together we took it out for our version of a camping trip, going to an uninhabited planet called Lleh Teswh. That was where Koji was killed.

We had been on Lleh Teswh four days when it happened. Put simply, we were attacked by Coryan pirates (the pirates that Fleet Intelligence insists do not exist). What they wanted most was our ship, the *Aerial*, and we were in a very remote area where no one would witness their piracy. The pirates struck when Koji and I were separated. I had gone looking for firewood on my own while Koji was inside the ship. I remember hearing a noise like a large animal coming through the thick piney bushes, and I paused, uncertain what to do about it. Then a big, helmeted humanoid male grabbed me from behind. We struggled, but he was almost half a meter taller than me and also skilled at hand-to-hand combat. I managed to shout a warning toward Koji before the air was knocked out of me and I collapsed to my knees. My short stature and delicate build obviously made him confident that a female wouldn't be difficult to dominate.

Gasping for breath, I wasn't able to resist much as magnetic cuffs were snapped onto my wrists and ankles. Then I was hoisted like a bag of rocks over this fellow's shoulder. I yelled feebly again to Koji, but my captor just chuckled as he carried me to an unfamiliar shuttle ship. There, he threw me inside without a word. My long red hair fell into my eyes and I couldn't see anything, but I could hear power weapons being fired outside. The magnetic cuffs not only restrained me, they adhered to the metal deck where I had landed, so I couldn't even sit up. Suddenly six or seven more helmeted humanoids scrambled into the ship around me and they fired up the ship's systems for liftoff. They knew I was totally unable to do anything to interfere with them, so I was shoved out of the way and ignored.

The deck in this shuttle ship was wide open, and I could see that they were chasing Koji, who had also lifted off in the *Aerial*. They could have shot him down easily, so I began to understand that they wanted the ship more than anything else. Knowing the capabilities of our ship, I was pretty confident that Koji could escape if he seriously tried to outrun them. However, I also knew that Koji was far too stubborn to run off and leave me at their mercy. He proved that when he turned the *Aerial* around and fired on them, obviously trying to bring them down. That startled the Coryans for a moment; our ship appeared to be a mere skimmer, and that type almost never carried weapons. However, Koji and I believed in precautions, and the *Aerial* was our prototype.

My captors' pilot uttered something I recognized as a Coryan oath as they banked sharply to avoid Koji's fire. Until that moment, I had no clue about their identities; they all still wore their mask-like helmets and I had been silently praying that they were not Wolfen. Learning that they were Coryan didn't make me feel much better. Their pilot maneuvered the shuttle around and then charged directly into Koji's fire. For a moment I thought we were all dead, until it became obvious that their ship had very good energy shields and all we did was rock around a bit. Koji started chasing us at that point, which seemed to amuse the Coryans immensely, judging from their laughter.

What ultimately happened must have been a malfunction aboard the *Aerial*, because the Coryans never fired back at him. Koji was an excellent pilot; nevertheless, he must have lost control and crashed into the rocky shoreline of a lake. The ship carrying me landed, and all but one of the pirates went to inspect the damage. They came back without Koji and immediately lifted off again. I knew then that he must be dead, either from the crash or at their hands.

I crouched very quietly on the deck, hiding my face in my arms, unable to keep from crying and yet trying not to attract attention. Koji and I had gone through the Academy together and we had loved each other for more than six years. I was incredibly, helplessly furious. If I had not been restrained by the cuffs, I think I might have killed those Coryans—or been killed trying. A rough hand in my hair pulled my head up, and the blue-helmeted pirate who had captured me stood above me with a blade in his free hand. I stared back up at the opaque faceplate of the helmet, willing myself not to cry out when he killed me. Then the pilot snarled something over his shoulder at the one holding me, and I was dropped like something hot. Moments later another one of them came near again and pushed a helmet over my head. It was only then that I realized I had been gasping for air. Atmospherics in their shuttles were apparently not as advanced as those in the Fleet.

Again, I was ignored. By watching the forward screen I could see that we had left the atmosphere of Lleh Teswh, and within a standard hour we were docked with a much larger ship, recognizable as a Coryan cruiser-raider class vessel. These guys were definitely pirates, probably smugglers.

After the docking procedures were completed, the cuffs were removed from my ankles and I was able to stand up. The helmet was then dragged off my head and I was taken into the main ship, all the while being yanked around by my blue-helmeted captor whom I had already begun to despise. We went down several winding corridors to what was obviously an officer's cabin. There I was presented to the captain, whose name I later learned was Chivv R. He was the first Coryan I had seen without a helmet; indeed, I had never before met a Coryan in the flesh. They are actually very handsome humanoids, with quite unusual coloring. Their skin is an incredible green that seems unreal.

Every Coryan I met on that ship (all males) had golden eyes. The youngest ones had dark green hair that looked almost black. Among those more mature, their hair color graduated to shades of lighter green. Their captain was only a head taller than me, but very wide across the shoulders—almost bull-like. He was in early middle age, as his hair was an earth-summer grass green, and he had intelligent, cold golden eyes. It amazed me when he addressed me in very good Standard speech, saying, "I am Chivv R, this ship's captain, and your name, Terran woman? What are you called?"

From the way he spoke to me I guessed they had no inkling of my Fleet affiliation. The durable camping clothing both Koji and I wore was quite civilian, and all of our identification tapes were locked away aboard the *Aerial* when it crashed. If they had found my ID, I'm certain I would have been killed immediately. When I hesitated before answering him, my original captor's big hand tightened on my collarbone, threatening to crush it, until Chivv R waved him off.

I managed to gasp out, "Honor. My name is Rose Honor." I had a surname, but I did not provide it. Honor is my middle name. *A friend began calling me Honor long ago, and I preferred it.*

"You will now forget your previous life, Rose Honor. If you are obedient to me, no harm will come to you on this ship. My crew obeys me. You are valuable property, and not to be injured if it can be avoided. If you were male, I might offer you the opportunity to prove yourself worthy of a place among my crew.

Unfortunately, birth left you female and you are therefore my lord's property to be protected until you are delivered to him. Do you understand me?"

Birth left me female? Trying to appear more awed than angry, I replied, "Yes, I think so." I did not like his use of the word "lord." It sounded like something Wolfen.

Chivv R gestured again and the man who had brought me to this cabin retreated quickly, leaving us alone. I could feel my heart racing, and not just with fear. Gossip in the Fleet always maintained that Coryan females had an incredibly powerful effect on human males, but it was never mentioned that Coryan males had a similar effect on human females. In spite of the anger and grief I felt for Koji, I could not help but react to the physical presence of this powerful Coryan male. I almost wished he would put on a helmet.

Apparently quite unaware of my involuntary physical reaction to him, Chivv R said coldly, "If you attempt escape, you will be killed without discussion. If you survive, your fate will be left to my lord when we reach Viste."

The deck was vibrating just a bit; the ship's engines were engaging. With an effort to remain calm, I asked, "Viste? I've never heard of it. Are we going there now?"

"We are," Chivv R affirmed, picking up a clear rod from a table. It looked like a weapon of some kind.

I flinched and backed against the wall. He smiled in rather cruel amusement and touched the manacles on my wrists. They fell off painlessly. "I keep my word," Chivv R said, "Remember that, female."

"Please," I whispered, my voice not as steady as I would have liked it to be, "I'm trying to understand my situation. I know you are . . . that your men wanted our ship. Why wasn't I killed like my companion?"

The male stepped closer and met my gaze evenly with those odd golden eyes. "There is a market for females in sectors not under your Fleet control. Human females are rare and quite a novelty so close to the Wolfen empire. You will undoubtedly bring us many prize credits." Then, half turning he called, "Renn Ce!"

The large Coryan with the blue helmet returned, this time holding the helmet under one arm. He was another incredible specimen, only taller and younger. By now my pulse felt like it should be audible in the little cabin. I hoped I wasn't blushing. The captain nodded toward me and Renn Ce's hand pulled me from the cabin. I was taken down a dim corridor, and then another, until at last he pushed me into a tiny cabin. My knees felt like soft wax as I backed away from him. His golden eyes were mocking as he shut the cabin door and I was left alone.

I collapsed onto the hard, narrow bunk, almost ready to laugh at myself. It now made sense to me why Coryan females were so incredibly desirable. Their males were apparently so cold that, if the females were not as they are their race probably would have ceased to exist long ago. For a while I sat and stared at the walls of the four-meter square cabin and thought about Koji. I wondered if there was any way he could have survived. Yet I knew there was none. I passed some time trying to think of how I might get out of this situation, but succeeded only in exhausting myself and falling asleep.

It took more than a standard month to reach planet Viste. I spent most of that time alone in the tiny cabin. I eventually learned that Viste is located in disputed space between the Wolfen, the Andree, and uncharted space. Wolfen patrols generally kept the Andree at bay, and vice versa. Piracy abounds there, with many crews running between the Wolfen patrols, or paying them off in prizes, or with bribery disguised as tribute.

During my incarceration in that confined space, I developed something of an obsession with performing simple calisthenics, just for something to do. There was very little else to pass the time, other than sleeping or mentally forming my report to Fleet Headquarters, should I escape the pirates. I wanted to stay in top physical shape in order to be ready when I saw an opportunity to act on my own behalf.

When the silent cabin door slid open that day, I lay on the cabin deck, catching my breath after my exercise routine. It took me a moment to realize that Renn Ce stood in the doorway, looking down at me. Another thing I learned about myself during this time was that after the initial pulse-jumping shock of looking one of these males in the eye, it was possible to dampen down my physical reaction to them. Nevertheless, I sat up quickly when I spotted him, controlling the urge to grab my blanket. I was in my thin underclothing.

His gaze seemed to be somewhat less impersonal this time. "What are you doing?" he demanded.

"Calisthenics," I replied quickly, and when he appeared puzzled by the word, I added, "Exercising. Why are you here?"

He stepped into the cabin. "We approach Viste. The captain wishes you brought to the bridge." Renn Ce held out a bundle of cloth to me. "You are to wear this."

Accepting the clothing, I glared impatiently at him and said, "Fine. May I have a moment alone to dress?"

Smiling unexpectedly, he said, "No." Then the Coryan reached forward and touched a loose strand of my hair, looking at it for a long moment.

I did not move, but my mind was racing over the possibilities.

Conversationally, he inquired, "Do many Terran women have hair this color? Like fiery embers?"

What a time for him to get interested, even poetic! "Yes," I replied, more calmly than I felt. "Other colors as well." I could feel my body wanting to react to his arrogant good looks, but a separate part of my mind was quickly calculating how seducing this pirate might tip the odds toward my escape.

"I have seen other human females," he remarked, "but none with hair this...red." He pulled me toward him suddenly, his mouth enveloping mine. His hands knew just where and how to touch me. To be honest, I slid willingly enough into his arms and physically enjoyed myself thoroughly. I doubt that I could have done much to stop him anyhow, and it had been a long, boring trip. Somewhat later, he let go of me abruptly and got up from the narrow bunk we had shared. "The captain is waiting," he said shortly. He was cold as space again.

Too tired just then to put up a fight, I got up quickly, shook out the long dark gown Renn Ce had given me and slipped it over my head. I fingered the tiny blue and silver crystals embroidered down its front. Was this what Coryan slaves were wearing this season on planet Viste? Trying not to shiver, I looked up at Renn Ce, wondering what the Coryan word for "bastard" was.

When we entered the bridge, Chivv R was speaking in Andree (a language I was fluent in, even then) to a member of that species on the viewer. I learned quickly that the conversation had to do with the recent death of Chivv's bandit lord. He had run afoul of the master of that port (actually of the entire planet, but I learned that later), a powerful being known as Drakyn.

Chivv's skin suddenly seemed a lighter green, akin to human pallor.

The high-pitched and distinct voice of the Andree went on, "It was a terrible thing to witness. Remak La thought he could cheat Drakyn, and of course Drakyn learned the truth. Then Remak was insane enough to attack the great Lord of Viste with a blaster. Drakyn took it away from him, forced the weapon into Remak's mouth and blew his head away. Remak La's men also died, most terribly. Their backs were broken with scarcely an effort from the monster. One of them came at Drakyn with a metal blade and got his own throat slashed for the effort. Oh, Fates! Drakyn drank his blood like ale!"

"A lie!" Chivv R suddenly exclaimed, but clearly he only wanted to be convinced.

"No, not a lie," the Andree said solemnly. "All of us are taking care not to upset the Lord of Viste now, not even to be noticed by him, at any cost. Most ships are trying to win his favor by bringing him remarkable females as gifts. It is said that he devours them like meat and bread, for they are never seen again. After the incident with Remak La, no one doubts this."

I wished I was invisible. I wished Wolfen warriors had captured me instead of these guys. Chivv turned thoughtful eyes toward me just then and I kept my face immobile. They did not know I understood Andree and I certainly was not about to enlighten them now.

After a moment, Chivv remarked, "We can do no less, then. Were any of the females offered to him Terran? From Earth?"

"Of course not," was the reply and the Andree seemed to notice me for the first time. "They're unheard of in this sector. I've never even seen one . . . Are you going to tell me you have one there?"

Chivv gestured and Renn pushed me closer to the viewer. "Indeed we have. I meant her as a prize gift for Remak La, but now it seems wiser to give her to Drakyn."

"Very wise, but two pities," the Andree remarked, staring at me. "One pity is the loss of credits, and another is that Drakyn will undoubtedly devour her."

"There is no profit to our own deaths," Chivv said solemnly.

My inclination was to agree with Chivv R's sentiments, but not with his plans for me. I was not being consulted in the matter, of course. It was difficult not to try and reason with him, but I knew that it would do no good at all and I did not want them to know I understood the conversation.

Turning to Renn Ce, Chivv R said in Coryan (which they knew I was now learning), "Take the female to the shuttle. I will join you there soon. You will accompany us to the surface. No others will go down yet."

Waiting for Renn Ce in the shuttle, I was somewhat relieved that they did not feel they must manacle me again. Renn was once more as distant as my home galaxy, so I knew no help would come from him. I was on my own. Deciding to play up my innocent act, I asked him, "The Andree your captain spoke with on the viewer, is he the 'Lord' Chivv R spoke of? Am I to be given to him?"

Renn Ce smiled in real amusement, and I could see the calculation taking place in his mind. He was torn between telling me the truth, to watch my reaction, or keeping me ignorant and more easily managed. His duty won and he replied, "The Andree was one of his agents."

I wanted to slap his handsome face. "What kind of place is Viste?" I pressed gently. My hands were shaking with rage, so I clasped them tightly in my lap to hide this. I tried to tell myself I had pretty much asked for what I got from him, but I was difficult to convince.

"It is a port," was his reply, "Much trading takes place."

Swell. Terrific. Marvelous, I thought, wanting to scream.

Soon Chivv R joined us, and Renn Ce piloted the shuttle down to an earth-like planet that appeared to be quite mountainous and heavily-wooded. There was a surprising amount of air traffic, and as we approached the architecture seemed rather feudal in style. I abruptly reminded myself, with a mental shake, that this was no Fleet-civilized planet. I had no idea what I might encounter here, but there would be no assistance for me from Fleet headquarters—no ambassadors, no prisoner exchange program, and certainly no rescue effort. If the Fleet believed I had survived at all, even if they suspected Coryan piracy, Fleet policy precluded any pursuit this deeply into the unexplored territories. I was certainly not important enough for any special attention.

However, I also knew that I absolutely refused to become any alien creature's main dinner dish, even metaphorically. Thus far I had presented a pliable and placid exterior to these pirates, and they obviously thought I was awed and frightened by my situation. Renn Ce was probably convinced that I now regarded him as someone special. I definitely hoped so. *Let them underestimate the silly Terran female!* I told myself.

The opportunity I had prayed for finally presented itself not long after we landed. We were in a huge shuttle hangar built into the side of a mountain, and the bay doors stood wide open to accommodate the constant traffic. Cold and damp wintry air blew in around us. A large collection of shuttles and other small craft were represented there, from the 10-man sized ships such as we had, down to single-being skimmers, not unlike the one Koji and I had designed, built, and flown. My attention was drawn in particular to a small two-seater craft in a far-off berth. Even in my worried and distracted state I could appreciate her design and style. It was a Fleet Hawk-type craft, and this little lovely probably had the capacity to really move at high speeds—something unusual in so small a ship back then.

Chivv R was occupied by the formalities of transferring cargo to the docks. Holding my breath, I made myself appear as small and nervous as possible, waiting for the one moment when the Coryans' attention was completely drawn away from me. At last that moment came during an argument about transport and docking fees. Chivv's voice had risen in supposed outrage, and Renn's grip on my arm had relaxed with his attention fully upon Chivv R.

It's now or never, I told myself, drawing in a deep and calming breath. The next few moments seemed like they moved in slow motion. I grabbed for Renn's blaster, connected, and pulled it from its holster even before he turned to me. I had already moved five steps away when I saw Chivv's weapon coming up. Without thinking, I fired the blaster at him from no more than ten meters away, and a huge bluish hole blossomed on his thigh.

Then I turned and ran like hell.

The startled faces of various alien races turned my way as I pounded the 300 meters to the little Hawk ship I wanted. No one stopped me. My luck held, and I was inside with the seals slammed shut and locked before I'd even taken a glance around to see if the ship was occupied. Thankfully, it was not. Again my luck held, as the ship's design was one I could activate blindfolded and pilot with a fingernail, if necessary.

Renn Ce's fist struck the side of the ship, but a blast of pressurized oxygen sent him reeling back in surprised pain. It was almost easy for me to push the little ship out of its berth, urging it upward. Just outside the bay doors, I met another ship's shuttle about to enter, and we nearly collided. However, I banked sharply to starboard and slipped by like a bird. Then I hit the thrusters with both fists and the Hawk leapt skyward. Knowing that I would surely be pursued, yet wary of territory I knew nothing about, I stayed within the atmosphere and leveled off at a low 20,000 meters. I was determined to evade any larger ship's pursuit using my small size and greater maneuverability. The amazingly-strong sensor system on board soon warned me of a larger ship emerging from the bay, but I still urged my little Hawk onward. Soon I would be out of any light shuttle ground sensor range.

About this time I noticed that there was too much ground traffic in the area, raising the possibility of a collision. With this in mind, I took a heading northward, away from the port city, but remained low enough to avoid most known scanning devices. Of course, I had no idea what kind of technology they used on this planet, but I could make assumptions from my own experience. My ship's sensors were able to make out a particular blip following my path and it appeared to be gaining on my vessel quickly. I estimated that my chances were now around 50/50, so I dropped lower and closer to the tree tops of an enormous forest below me. I could see two mountain peaks rising ahead—snowy peaks shining in the planet's yellow sun.

The blip was getting larger and closer now. Its weapons would probably outstrip any on this little ship... or would they? Recklessly, I activated the forward and then the aft weapons banks and was startled by the energy readings that registered on the control board. Those chances were now 65/35—in my favor!

I was getting excited. Koji was always better at performing the attack maneuver I had in mind, but he was an excellent teacher. Smiling to myself, I turned the craft around in a tight arc and went to face that damned Coryan blip, which was now at a higher altitude. Locking my laser guns the moment the other ship came into range, I kept a light touch on the navigational stick.

The Coryan shuttle came lumbering my way like an angry goat, but the Hawk came up under its belly, Terran shark-style, and burnt away the ship's outer shielding in a long, surgical hit. I leaned on the laser switch until I saw the shuttle begin to belch smoke and sparks. After another roll, I waited until my tail section faced the Coryan and then I fired the rear banks at Renn Ce's wounded underside again. The shuttle shattered like brittle glass, sending huge chunks of burning metal and plastic in all directions, including directly at my Hawk. Then and only then did I realize that my craft had absolutely no functioning energy shields. No wonder it was docked!

The explosion neatly sheared off my rear thrusters, taking with them almost all of my maneuvering ability. The forest came rushing up at me with alarming speed, and I fought to engage the forward thrusters to slow my fall. Before I could decide if it was going to work, a tall pine tree interfered with everything and I heard a terrible cracking sound. Moments later I lost consciousness.

Darkness. Pain. Cold. More darkness. I cannot move any part of my body. There is movement near me; someone touches me, resulting in searing pain down my back. I try to scream, but I have little breath; I feel like I am drowning. The pain disappears suddenly, but the cold seems to grow deeper.

Movement again. I am being lifted up through the cold, cold air, but I am happy because the pain is gone. There is wetness on my face—tears, or perhaps blood. After a monumental effort I manage to open my eyes, but there is redness before them and I am blind. Something gently touches my forehead and eyes. I can see again, but only dimly because it is so dark. A voice fills my head . . . or is it from inside me? Deep and commanding, it says, "You will look at me. Clear your brain of its confusion and regard me honestly. Now!"

Unable to resist the order, I blink twice and then I am able to focus my eyes on a face just above mine. Human, it is unmistakably a humanoid male. Terran? I want to swallow the liquid in my mouth but I cannot, so it flows out over my lips. Dark, blue-black eyes bore into mine and again I hear words: "There is more to you than a simple thief of ships. Why did you steal and flee?"

Struggling again, I cannot make myself speak. Instead, images of what happened to me with the Coryans, and their intentions for me, are drawn swiftly from my mind to . . . his mind. I am completely honest, even about who and what I am.

The voice seems less harsh now. "You were yourself a victim, stolen from your life and your duty. But not quite the helpless creature they supposed. You are dying. How badly do you wish to live?"

Once more the only answers I can offer are drawn directly from my mind without words. My eyesight is blurring, failing again. Fear nibbles at my thoughts. I cling mentally to the sound of that rich voice, promising anything and everything. A sensation of warmth begins gradually at the side of my throat, dispelling the cold and relieving the pain. Quite literally, I feel myself slowly and delightfully consumed by the owner of that incredible voice.

Chapter 2

Drakyn's Compulsion

DRAKYN, the dreaded Lord in control of planet Viste, was in his castle-like fortress that day. This was where he spent most of his time, disliking the administrative offices and the bustle of people in the port. Nevertheless, his computers monitored most activities, and he was immediately notified of the theft of his ship from its berth. Theft was almost unheard of in this port, despite the abundance of pirates and other enterprising beings from many planets that frequented the place. It was well-known how harshly Drakyn dealt with thieves of any sort. This severity made even the worst of enemies hesitate to accuse each other of dishonesty here.

    Drakyn was an impressive male humanoid dwelling among these mostly-alien life forms. His physical size was only slightly above the norm for humanoids, but his regal bearing, intensely dark blue eyes, and incredible physical strength made him more than a challenge to any being on Viste. He had controlled the settlements on that mountainous and remote planet longer than anyone kept records, and no one dared challenge his claim to rule all who came there.

    Everyone feared him, even those with whom he chose to associate himself for business reasons. Most of the time Drakyn kept himself in solitude, even within the massive fortress dwelling that had been carved out of the side of a mountain not far from the port. Those who served him loyally seldom had anything to complain about, while those foolish enough to plot or plan against him were invariably discovered and dealt with most terribly.

Pried ker D'at, the blue-skinned Andree who had known him and served as Master of the Port for many years, often wondered silently about the Lord, for he never spoke of his past or of any family ties. When questioned, Drakyn merely said that they were all gone. The Andree were an extremely family-oriented people, and Drakyn's aloneness made the aging administrator pity Drakyn on some levels, but he feared and admired him even more.

Astonishment was evident in the Andree's high-pitched voice as Pried reported to Drakyn via the link, "Someone's stolen your two-being ship from berth 8/432! It must be some lunatic. The Coryan shuttle that just landed—their captain has been wounded and his attacker escaped in *8/432*. The Coryan will undoubtedly destroy the ship, my lord!"

Moving quickly to a monitor of his own, Drakyn keyed up the air traffic screens to observe the pursuit himself, experiencing a strange sense of unease, quite unusual for him. He knew himself well enough to take heed of his own premonitions. "Is there any information on the thief?" Drakyn snapped at the Andree, who was busy on the comlink obtaining it.

"The Coryan captain, one Chivv R, merely reports it as a captive female. Her ability to pilot a ship was unknown to him," was Pried's reply.

Observing the very tight chase that the thief was leading, Drakyn's sense of unease became absolutely intense. "Ready my own ship," he ordered suddenly, heading for the door. Drakyn was certain that whoever flew *8/432* had very little time left to live if he did not act. On one level he wondered why it mattered to him at all, but on another he was certain that he did care—quite intensely!

Within a few ticks of time, he had lifted off in one of his own ships, one of similar size and power as that of the stolen *8/432*, and he was easily able to tune his sensors to the chase in progress. The female who had stolen the ship was coming in Drakyn's direction, and when the opportunity presented, he would capture the thief himself. Even as he made this decision, his uneasy feeling became almost an overwhelming emotion, a worry that he could not explain. Drakyn loved neither man nor beast. His encounters with females found on or around Viste were arranged only to satisfy his physical needs, and they were never more than dalliances quickly forgotten. He did not understand this inexplicable concern for some unknown female slave—she could be no more than that because he knew the Coryan pirates would have a female aboard for no other reason. He grew inordinately curious about this female!

Pushing away his unruly thoughts, he observed the little *8/432* being taken through evasive maneuvers for which it had not been designed. The pilot was doing her best to escape the pursuing Coryan ship and her efforts demonstrated great piloting skills, as well as desperation of the kind that encouraged dangerous risk taking. The thief was certainly an able pilot; therefore, she would not be Coryan. That race seldom even taught their females to read. Ramping down his temper, Drakyn resolved to at least hear the female's story before acting for or against the talented thief. He observed what happened on his tracking screen. The small shuttle would soon be caught by the Coryan ship. Just then, however, the tiny ship's pilot chose to make a courageous move, coming up under the bigger ship's belly and firing blasts at close range. Following this, she rolled it over and fired her aft cannons for good measure, shattering much of the bigger shuttle's underside. However, huge pieces of the disintegrating shuttle struck the aft thruster area of *8/432*, destroying any ability to maneuver the fleeing ship.

Automatically, Drakyn reached out to catch and experience the emotions of the thief. He expected to pick up great terror from the occupant of *8/432* as she crashed into a grove of huge pine trees near the top of the mountain. He was startled to merely sense surprise, frustration, and even irritation before blackness overtook the female thief. A Coryan had ejected from the pursuing shuttle ship. Drakyn knew he would soon be retrieved by the patrols already in pursuit. However, he was not interested in the Coryan. He directed his own ship to the crash site and within ten ticks he put down near the twisted, smoldering wreck that had been *8/432*.

The smell of wet pine needles and electrical smoke filled the air as Drakyn climbed out of his ship and regarded the remains of his little shuttle. He surveyed the mess without any emotion beyond continuing curiosity. Approaching the ship, Drakyn saw a tiny figure still inside the ruin, lying against what had been the control console. From her small size, he thought for a moment it might actually be a child. He easily bent back the shards of hot metal trapping her within the shuttle. Her whole head was covered with blood, so he used a corner of his cloak to wipe her face and assess any injury there.

When he uncovered and gazed upon her delicate features, he suddenly felt as if the very breath in his lungs had somehow been frozen to complete stillness. In utter immobility, he simply stared. Then she moaned softly in pain, and he quickly touched her wrist to judge how much physical damage had been done. For some reason his hands trembled slightly. Then something moved within Drakyn's chest. It was something that had been dormant for more years than he cared to count, and thus this movement, this activation was something alarming, even painful to endure. After a brief, internal struggle Drakyn moved decisively to free the pinned woman's body from the interior of the crashed shuttle ship.

When he lifted her free, her weak scream was involuntary and agonized. Drakyn quickly covered her eyes with his hand and used his considerable mental ability to block the knowledge of pain from her brain. Moving swiftly but deliberately, he lay her down upon the cool grass and examined her entire body carefully, concerned by the extent of the damage. Her spine was seriously injured and both of her legs had multiple fractures. Internal organs that served vital functions were ruptured, and she was hemorrhaging. There was very little time remaining for this little human female, and it would be kind to simply continue to block her pain for the few remaining moments of her life.

Yet somehow, against all reason and possibility, Drakyn could not allow her to die. Somehow Drakyn knew this woman—this complete stranger. On a level close to cellular, he had always known his fate was interwoven with the fate of this total stranger whose beautiful features had haunted his dreams for many lonely centuries. Regarding her now, his long-dormant emotions awakened, tasting at first of longing and then loss. Finally, they somehow bloomed into a strange sort of relief and a promise of joy.

Again he asserted control over himself and forced internal calm, as he lifted her hand and tasted the blood smeared there. He was surprised and alarmed to realize that she was not of his racial background. This female was completely Terran-human, and though not yet in her thirtieth year of life, she was dying. He was vaguely aware of his own comlink squawking questions at him from his ship as he leaned over the stricken woman, silently commanding her to open her eyes. Slowly she did so, blinking away blood with her tears. Without using a spoken word, he commanded, *You will fix your gaze upon me. Clear your brain of its confusion and regard me honestly. Now!*

He observed her confusion and felt her fear as she struggled against her weakening body to obey him. Her lips moved but no sound emerged, only bubbles of blood as she tried to breathe. The canines were aching in his jaw as he demanded information from her; he must be certain before he acted! The woman was unable to speak, but Drakyn drew the images of her past directly from her unguarded thoughts. She made no effort to resist his inquiry. Soon he realized that she was innocent of any real crime. Trustingly, she surrendered more information about herself than was wise for a vulnerable female with any stranger.

When he realized that she had been abducted, Drakyn's ice-bound heart actually pained him for a moment. He spoke aloud now, saying, "You were yourself stolen, then. But not quite the helpless creature the Coryans supposed. Your injuries are serious, woman. You are dying. How badly do you wish to live?"

Her powerful yearning for freedom, her joy for life itself, struck Drakyn's atrophied emotions like a hand slapping his face. He actually recoiled for a moment before deliberately leaning closer to the woman, instructing her brain to relax and to trust him. Again he felt her confusion and fear as she sank downward toward what she perceived was approaching death. Her brain instinctively reached out for his, assuming he would assist and support her.

Drakyn silently soothed her and reassured her that all would be well, even as he allowed his canine teeth to extend themselves fully. Then he held the unconscious female in his arms like a lover as he sunk his fang-like teeth into the big vein barely visible in her white throat. The tiny moan she uttered thrilled him just as much as the intoxicating perfume and taste of her young, sweet blood. He drank deeply, not even realizing one of his hands was caressing her pale cheek.

***

TARQUIN, Port Viste's Security Chief and a huge gray cat-like felinoid of the Malkin race, had followed the two ships from the port. He had also observed the pursuit and subsequent battle between these ships, and it did not surprise him in the least to witness the culmination of this incident. He directed his ground forces to the damaged Coryan ship, and proceeded personally toward the crashed 8/432. Pried ker D'at had contacted Tarquin via the comlink and informed him of Drakyn's personal attention to the incident, and Tarquin's instruments also tracked Drakyn's arrival at the crash scene several ticks prior to his own. Experience with how the Lord of Viste dealt with thieves made Tarquin prepare himself for a very unpleasant scene when he touched down near the crash site.

By the time Tarquin had landed, Drakyn was preparing to take flight again. Seeing Tarquin land, Drakyn came back out of his ship and approached him. Nodding toward the still-smoking vessel, Drakyn said, "Have a crew remove this wreck and take it back to the docking area. Leave it on display there without cleaning or covering it, as a warning to anyone who might be inclined to steal my property in the future."

Nodding immediate assent, Tarquin's sensitive nostrils filled with the scent of newly-spilled humanoid blood. He could see it was splattered inside the ruined ship, on a flattened area of grass near their feet, and that the front of Drakyn's tunic was soaked with it. Swallowing to control his urge to be sick, Tarquin carefully inquired, "What of the pilot—the thief—Lord Drakyn?"

Drakyn had already turned away from the felinoid, but he paused and replied, "I have the thief. That person is not your concern. Do not pursue the matter further, and advise the Coryans on the wisdom of forgetting that the female ever existed." He glanced strangely back at Tarquin as if about to say more, but then turned away again.

Deeply appalled, Tarquin had no intention of asking more

questions. The majority of the blood around here was wet enough and fresh enough to indicate that the female thief had survived the crash. Tarquin felt sincere pity for the thief, but turned his mind away from considering what Drakyn might inflict upon this female humanoid who had dared to offend him in this manner. Returning promptly to his ship, Tarquin used the comlink to immediately dispense Drakyn's orders.

Drakyn took his craft away from that place of near-death and piloted it back to his mountain fortress. Guiding the ship skillfully, he headed directly to the secluded hangar he had built at the base of the sheer cliffs on the northern face, a kilometer below the castle. Long, dark tunnels led back up to the fortress itself, but few knew of their existence, and he had given his staff direct orders never to venture there without his company. He berthed his ship, closed the shielded doors behind himself and locked down the craft's systems. Then Drakyn turned to the tiny female figure he had carefully laid out on the deck beneath his feet. Her spine had been meticulously manipulated into the correct position for re-growth of damaged nerves and fractured bones, and her broken legs had been pulled straight and bound tightly so they could not be jarred. They would heal themselves properly. However, she remained hovering at the edges of physical death; the internal damage now needed his attention and radical intervention.

Drakyn caught hold of the pilot seat he had just vacated, grasped it with both hands and tore the chair from its moorings with one swift movement. He did the same with the seat intended for the co-pilot, and tossed both damaged chairs aft, out of his way. He would need room and the ship could be repaired at a later time. Now Drakyn stood above the senseless woman, slipped off his heavy cloak and dropped to his knees beside her body. Using a sharp blade, he cut away the remnants of her torn black slave's robe, discarding the pieces of cloth toward the portal to be burned later. His mind was so intent upon his work that he did not pause to consider how unusual it was for him to treat another being with such care and gentleness. Her mind was now completely under his control. She would not experience any more pain, despite what he might do to facilitate the change. The blood had stopped flowing from her hundreds of cuts and abrasions now, but her pulse was almost non-existent.

Drakyn's glacial eyes scanned the female's compact, athletic body, searching for injuries that might have been overlooked previously. His body thrummed with a strange kind of tension that was at once both sexual and somehow spiritual in nature, but he could not pause yet to consider what this meant. He ripped open his own stained tunic and picked up a small cup-like vessel with his left hand while still holding the blade in his right. Then he cut open the large vein just above his heart, slashing deeply enough that his blood poured forth freely and spilled into the cup he held ready. Then he pressed his hand over his own wound and commanded it to close itself immediately. With a grim smile, Drakyn then leaned over the woman and poured a few drops of his own blood into each of her open wounds, emotionlessly watching as each cut and contusion folded itself together and the skin sealed immediately without a scar. His blood would heal her internal injuries, as well, but those would require more time. It had been many, many years since he had done this for anyone. He had sworn never to do so again and forced himself to forget the circumstances surrounding that oath. Drakyn was absolutely compelled by the overpowering mix of emotion and desire that this female evoked in him, which led him to take this action. He was certain that her survival was somehow necessary for his own future.

When the last of the open wounds had seamlessly closed, Drakyn sat back on his heels, and just gazed at her for several moments. She was no longer a Terran human; she was now more like Drakyn than any female born of Drakyn's own race. For her sake, he hoped that she would adapt well to her new form of life; if she did not, he might be forced to destroy her one day. He now allowed himself to examine her incredibly lovely face. When he lightly caressed the curves of her features and the fullness of her silent lips, Drakyn doubted that she could bring him anything less than future joy.

Shaking himself out of such an unusual reverie, Drakyn reminded himself forcibly that it would be several months before she could be allowed to return to consciousness. It would take a long time for her broken bones and internal injuries to heal, and until that time it was his duty to see to her every physical need. He did not want to move her until he was certain that her spine was properly healing, so he tended to her on the floor of his shuttle ship for more than twenty days. He spent most of that time at her side, as he needed to be in near-constant physical contact with her to maintain control over the pain blocks. Not once did he allow her even near consciousness. Her reaction to the pain that would inevitably return with awareness could do new damage, and even bring on madness.

Many days later, Drakyn became aware that his people in the fortress, and even in the port offices, had begun wondering what so fascinated Drakyn down in his shuttle hangars. Eventually a rumor surfaced that he was using that area as his personal torture chamber. That rumor undoubtedly originated about a week after the crash, when Tarquin called him on the comlink about an urgent matter. Drakyn came up immediately from the hangars and Tarquin met him at the doorway. There was fresh blood on the Lord's bared chest and hands. Tarquin did not know that the blood was Drakyn's own, and that he had been transfusing it into the woman's veins for nourishment. Tarquin had not commented on the blood, and he was not inclined to ask questions of Drakyn. Thus, it was easy to assume something more sinister.

The rumor entertained Drakyn when he overheard it in a conversation between two of his felinoid security guards. He made no effort to correct or dispel the story, as it only added to the fear and respect afforded to him. It also kept them at a distance from him, which was as he liked it. Even more humorous to Drakyn was the day he summoned Tarquin, instructing him to bring along a strong companion and meet him at the mountain hangar area. The two felinoids appeared promptly, but their ears were laid back in honest worry.

Drakyn did not show his amusement with their distress, but merely nodded back toward his shuttle and said, "There is a humanoid female inside the ship. She is seriously damaged and unconscious. I want her carried, very carefully, up to the fortress above and into my chambers. Come now."

Their fur stood up slightly at the back of their necks as Tarquin and his friend Gellin entered the shuttle, expecting to see awful things. It calmed them somewhat when they beheld the peaceful sight of a small female wrapped in layers of pristine white cloth, deeply unconscious. At Drakyn's direction, the female was carefully moved on to a stretcher, secured to it, and then taken from the shuttle and up the several flights of stairs into the castle. Molecular transporters existed on Viste, but they did not ask Drakyn why he chose not to use one for this move.

In the castle corridors, people they met fled out of their path, not daring to even peek out at the procession as Drakyn led the way. The stern expression on his face entirely forbade conversation. When they reached Drakyn's private rooms, he had them transfer the female to his own huge bed and then he abruptly dismissed them.

The heavy wooden door shut after them and the two felinoids were silent until they had gone down an entire flight of stairs. Then the younger felinoid remarked to his friend, "The Lord of Viste seems to treasure this female, Tarquin."

Shaking his shaggy head, Tarquin licked his own shoulder nervously before replying, "Who can tell, my friend? It is never wise to examine Lord Drakyn's motivations too closely."

Drakyn continued to keep watch over and personally tend to the senseless female's needs for more than one hundred additional days and nights. He only left his chambers to eat, and once he had obtained the necessary protein, Drakyn returned immediately back to his chambers.

Tarquin made it his personal business to watch the stairs leading up to Drakyn's private wing. It seemed significant to him that Drakyn had apparently lost interest in the many willing females staffing the fortress. He sensed that the female thief was at the bottom of this mystery, but he was at a loss to explain why. Despite the widespread rumors of torture, Tarquin was certain that Drakyn was unaccountably enamored of the female. For her own sake, Tarquin hoped she would return Drakyn's interest.

When not tending to the woman's care, Drakyn spent much of his time seated before the cavernous fireplace in his chambers. His mind roiled with images that he had become convinced were memories of some kind. Her face, and the low and gentle voice he was certain belonged to her, were there with him whether he was awake or asleep. These impossible memories apparently had something to do with his deliberately-forgotten life one thousand solar years past. If he had a superstitious nature he might have been inclined to believe witchcraft of some kind was involved, but he knew far too much of nature and science to give that a second thought.

He could see that the woman was growing stronger. At times she moved her arms and legs like a restless sleeper. This was a good sign that all was healing properly within her body.

Drakyn had actually been sleeping in his chair the day that the woman finally returned to awareness. His mental blocks against consciousness had been relaxed for more than a week in anticipation of her awakening. At the first sound of her soft moan, Drakyn snapped to full wakefulness himself and turned his eyes toward the huge bed. She was moving restlessly, pulling at the gauze still encasing her face and body.

Silently, he stood at the foot of the bed and watched awareness return to her. She had raised her hand to her face, and then her hand stopped moving as she held it motionless before her amazingly green eyes. Finally the hand dropped back to her side, and she stared upward at the vaulted ceiling for a few heartbeats.

Drakyn remained silent, allowing her to orient herself within her body again; he waited for her to see him.

Chapter 3

Awakening

EVERY possible inch of my body was a burning ache. I moved my hand and found my skin was wrapped in some sort of soft cloth. It took an effort, but I opened my eyes and blinked until I was able to focus on a high beamed stone ceiling above me. I lay on a firm, but yielding surface. I could not quite shake off my confusion. *What had happened to me?* Panic welled up inside. I heard myself moan. *Control, control,* I counseled myself. *Take deep breaths. The oxygen will help you think.* I managed to raise a hand and squint at it, finding it swaddled in cloth like an Egyptian mummy.

"Koji?" I murmured questioningly, "Koji, are you there?" Where in space was he? Where was I, and what was I wrapped in? Were these some kind of bandages? Fumbling, I pulled the cloth away from my mouth. "Koji?" I called again.

A cellar-deep yet musical voice spoke up from beyond my line of vision: "Your lover is dead, Honor. Calm your mind and allow the memories to return. Your body is recovered and whole once again."

My body gave a start at the sound of the voice, catching my breath. Just that quickly all of my memories returned: Koji's death, the Coryan pirates, my captivity and escape, and the crash. Only the events immediately following the crash remained a mental jumble.

Dimly, I could now see a human figure coming toward me, the bright light from a window behind him made it difficult to perceive any details. He seemed very tall and broad in the shoulders, but I could not see his face yet. Then, the voice I suddenly remembered from after the crash spoke again, "Now you recall, do you not?"

Something about him frightened me badly, making me think of death, of falling into a void. I moved over to the edge of the bed, intending to jump to my feet and run, but I found my legs were as weak as an infant's and I fell sprawling onto the stone floor near the bed.

Amusement sounded in his calm voice: "I was about to tell you to move slowly and deliberately in these first moments. You are well again and in no pain. Your strength will return swiftly. Grasp my hand, Honor."

I really did not want to touch him, but his voice was terribly compelling somehow, like an audible drug to my senses. In spite of myself, I lifted a hand and placed it in his, letting his strength draw me slowly and shakily to my feet before him. He towered over me. I looked up into dark blue eyes like polished sapphire and felt myself trembling. He was definitely humanoid, with an arrestingly handsome face framed by smooth black hair that fell down to his wide shoulders. He was clean-shaven, but a hint of blueness outlined his square, stubborn jaw. His face seemed stern and unapproachable, but he was compellingly attractive. There was also an air of aristocracy about him; a kind of power and assurance. He was in command of himself and accustomed to expecting obedience from others.

I suddenly felt extremely self-conscious, like an awkward child. Tearing my gaze away from his, I looked down at myself and saw that I was wrapped everywhere in the white cloth. Wondering aloud I asked, "Was I hurt that badly?"

"Indeed you were," he replied, his voice a low rumble. "You would most certainly have died without my intervention. There is no longer any danger of death. The cloth may now be discarded for more traditional coverings." He then began to remove the material enclosing my head and shoulders, dropping the pieces to the floor.

"Please," I breathed, only too aware of my complete helplessness and wanting to flinch away from his touch and what it was making me feel. "Please, I…"

"Yes?" He responded, becoming very still and fixing his incredible eyes on my face.

"I-I was very frightened after the crash. In pain. I-I promised you…"

A startling, white smile flashed on that sober face and the eyes seemed to be sending heat wherever his vision touched me. "You did."

My heart fluttered like it wanted out of my chest; I could scarcely hear him over its pounding. If he would have moved in that moment, I would have screamed and become completely hysterical with fear. Wisely, he was motionless, watching me steadily.

After an interminable moment, he asked in a cold voice: "Was it only fear? I have told you, I dislike thieves. I will not knowingly take anything unwillingly surrendered, not even from you, my little thief. You are not in pain or under duress now, Honor."

Again we regarded each other without words. Almost cautiously, he extended his hand and his fingertips traced a light and gentle line along my jaw down to the pulse in my throat.

As though in an instant, I became calm. Without words I suddenly and simply knew everything about him and I understood him and trusted him. Nothing was withheld by him. It was a complete opening of his mind and heart, and realized I could trust him. I was safe and secure in his presence. Surely, I belonged here.

"Anything," I whispered, "Everything." Stepping forward into his sheltering arms, I reiterated, "Everything, Drakyn…"

I also knew he was Drakyn, the monster and drinker of blood. Yet it did not matter.

Chapter 4

Anything...

THOUGH the woman had fallen to the floor, Drakyn could not reach down and scoop her up as he desired. She was on the edge of complete panic. Her every sensation was magnified by the profound change in her physicality. He knew he must handle her with extraordinary patience and extreme care. He used his most compelling voice to assuage the fear that rose from her skin like smoke. At last she reached out her small hand and placed it into his outstretched one, and he drew her easily to her feet. She was visibly trembling from more than her weakness, yet her clear green eyes fastened upon his face with a power of their own, seeming to examine him critically enough to make him feel unexpectedly self-conscious. *What sort of monster did she see?* he wondered.

He reassured her again that she had fully recovered from her injuries and then began again to remove the protective cloth from her body. He wanted to offer her the beautiful clothing he had prepared for her use. However, her fear stopped him. Her eyes revealed a compelling depth of vulnerability, so he immediately halted, suddenly realizing that his actions could be misinterpreted as sexual advances.

He released her hand and looked down at her lovely face, feeling a sudden physical desire that startled his body and his mind with its strength. He clenched his fists to keep from grabbing her and forcing her to yield to the kind of passion he felt, and instead carefully controlled the desire that had been building during these many days and nights caring for her body.

She whispered, "I-I was very frightened. In pain. I-I promised you...?"

Unable to keep from smiling at the memory of that short link within her mind, Drakyn merely said, "You did." Watching the changing emotions fleeting across her features, Drakyn did not move. He sensed that his slightest gesture could panic her and drive her into a foolish flight from him.

Exerting a great effort to keep his tone detached and calm, Drakyn knew his voice was too reserved. He again attempted to reassure her that he would not force her to do anything against her will. He stared at her, not allowing his face to show the worried emotions he was experiencing himself in those moments.

Then as if a veil had been lifted from her eyes, Honor's gaze softened upon him and she smiled slightly, impossibly, as though she, too, was also recognizing him from some long-forgotten past acquaintance. She was suddenly calm and assured. "Anything," she whispered, delighting him completely by offering him both hands, "Everything."

He opened his arms to her, trembling slightly himself the first moment she fitted her tiny frame against his. He closed his arms around her as her lips brushed against his throat. "Everything, Drakyn!" she repeated. Her hands were now against his chest, sliding up around his neck and clinging there willingly. With more than mere trust, she now offered him the universe.

Lowering his head, Drakyn's mouth found and claimed hers. He intended the kiss to be gentle, but it rapidly built into something quite different. Their passion grew as the kiss went on and on. He did not want to hurt her in any way, and he was gratified when she held on happily as he lifted her from her feet and carried her back to the bed. Between continued kisses he removed the gauze from her body until once again he was able to see the perfection of her skin. Honor made no false gestures of modesty, and she seemed to have literally discarded any fear of him. For the first time in many years, his body desired much more than a physical coupling. He wanted and needed to make this woman crave him as much as he did her. His hands and his lips worshipped her entire body until he felt her desire rising to meet his own.

With similar feelings, Honor responded to him and opened for him like a sweetly blooming flower. Their union was far more than mutual pleasure.

Chapter 5

Drakyn's Lady

EVERYTHING, including life itself, now seemed very strange to me. The overwhelming fear I had experienced upon waking in Drakyn's fortress had been replaced with a kind of passion so intense that it bewildered and overwhelmed me. Later, when I was alone, and I could again think dispassionately, I was reminded of descriptions of how people became seduced in the grip of a magical spell. I did not believe in magic spells, so I shook myself mentally and laughed away these briefly troubling thoughts.

Closing my eyes, I felt a new wave of desire for the man. Drakyn had spent literally hours holding me, alternating between gentle lovemaking and demonstrations of ferocious and passionate stamina. He seemed to sense whatever I needed, and he acted to fulfill that need even before the desire fully formed in my mind. I had never before experienced anything as intense as the climaxes his hands, mouth, and body had repeatedly created between us in those hours. The sun was shining when he had first kissed my mouth, and we continued our love play throughout the darkness of the night until the first rays of morning light turned the skies pink and yellow.

It was then that Drakyn scooped me up in his arms and walked over to the huge window. Holding me securely in his strong arms, we watched the sun rise together. Finally, he kissed the top of my head and said, "You are mine now, my lady, and this place will be your home."

At that moment I was entirely too deliciously content and sleepy to take issue with this masculine need to *own* me, but I filed the thought away for future discussion. Instead, I merely remarked, "I have never wanted to belong to any man, Drakyn. I enjoy my freedom."

"Sleep, little one," he said soothingly, with his magnetic, dark voice. "You and I have always needed each other and searched for each other without even knowing we did so. Surely you feel that as well…"

"I do," I admitted, nestling my head against his muscular shoulder, smiling as I realized distantly that my words were the customary response to a wedding vow. I drifted away into sleep still wrapped in his arms, but wanting to say more—wanting to point out that I was a commissioned officer of the Fleet, and that I had duties and responsibilities elsewhere. Instead, I slept.

When I awakened again I was alone in the big bed, still nude, and lying under a luxurious fur blanket. For a long time I just lay there, remembering and savoring how Drakyn had touched my body. Finally curiosity about my "new home" got the better of me, so I sat up and looked around the big room. The walls were composed of gray cut stone, and there was the huge fireplace I recalled from yesterday. The furniture was all made of heavy black wood, intricately carved and ancient looking. It reminded me of medieval museum pieces I had seen on Earth.

Wrapping a blanket around myself, I got out of bed and went through an open door where I found a huge bath area with a massive black stone tub and a functioning shower. I was delighted to notice that a long white gown of rich fabric, embroidered down the front with green and gold threads, had been laid out over a nearby chest. They lay together with heavy, thick cloths that I guessed were used as towels here on Viste. I chose to shower just then and enjoyed scrubbing my body and my hair, which had grown much longer than it was before my injuries. This made me wonder just how long I had been unconscious after that crash.

I finished quickly and got into the white gown, though I would have preferred trousers and a shirt, and then I combed out my hair while sitting in the sunshine that slanted into the room through the big windows. It was about this same time yesterday that I had first awakened in this room. I shivered slightly and began to wonder about other things, like what had become of Chivv R and Renn Ce. Had they survived their own crash? Would I ever get away from this place, back to the Fleet? Somehow, I doubted that Drakyn would arrange a ride home for me. More importantly, did I really want to go back?

Almost on cue with my thoughts, the big wooden door opened and Drakyn, Lord of Viste, swept into the chamber, his long black cloak hanging like wings from his broad shoulders.

"Did you sleep well, Honor?" he greeted me, shutting the door firmly and turning a key.

More sharply than I intended, I demanded, "Am I your prisoner in this room, Drakyn?" I tried not to think of how my heart had sped up at the sight of him.

"Do I need to imprison you?" he countered, his tone ironic. He looked at me with those night-dark eyes, his sensuous mouth turned down at the corners in slight irritation. The width of his shoulders and his aggressive way of standing with feet planted firmly should have intimidated me. Instead the sight of him made me tremble inside, but not from any kind of fear.

A bit puzzled, I imitated his stance, putting my hands on my hips and said, "I hope not, Drakyn, but I suspect that if anyone could make me enjoy captivity, it would be you. I wish I-I understood…all of this…" I gestured vaguely around the room.

"You shall, Honor. I promise you. But can you not simply enjoy the moment for now?" He then deliberately relaxed his posture, leaning back against the closed door with arms crossed over his chest, smiling at me.

He reminded me at the moment of a wild and unpredictable predator. The big chamber seemed much smaller with him inside it, and he looked at me with such obvious desire that a shudder ran down my spine, followed immediately by an unexpected rush of strange, painful hunger that actually made me stagger a bit. I blinked at him in alarm.

Calmly, Drakyn stepped toward me and said, "Don't be frightened by what you are feeling. You simply require nourishment, Honor. My people have prepared a meal for us. The injuries you suffered and the manner in which they were healed have changed you greatly. What you require to survive and thrive is vastly different from your previous lifestyle. You must continue to trust me, little one." A blade appeared in his hand and he used it to cut across his own wrist, ignoring my protest. He then offered that bleeding wrist to me, saying, "You need this first."

The sight of the blood made me act instinctively rather than with any kind of prescient thought. Before I knew what I was doing, I had grabbed his arm and leaned over the crimson fluid. Pressing my lips tightly over the wound, I began drawing the blood eagerly into my mouth and swallowing as if it was the finest wine. Then I suddenly realized exactly what I was doing! I dropped his arm and staggered back from Drakyn in real alarm.

He did not move from where he stood, but I continued backing away from him until my shoulders came into contact with the stone wall near the window. I put my hands against the cold wall, gasping against the unsatisfied hunger that was powerfully rearing within me. I could feel my control slipping away as the craving overtook me in compelling waves of desire that my newly-initiated and confused brain still interpreted as danger—as evil. With one trembling hand I pressed my own stomach as if to communicate with some alien thing within it, to tell it that it did not belong there and I would not be controlled by its demands.

"What is this? What have I become? What have you DONE to me?" I demanded anxiously, flinching at the sound of the fear bordering on loathing in my own voice. I scrubbed a hand over my mouth, expecting to be sick at any moment, but I was not. Indeed, my body felt wonderful; all of my senses seemed heightened, almost as if I had ingested a drug.

Drakyn was calmly wrapping a piece of cloth around his own wrist, his expression unreadable.

"You've made me a vampire? No, I will not have this! I'm not about to sleep in a coffin and walk around after dark looking for victims!" I was now growing a bit wild with fear.

"Of course not," Drakyn agreed, "You're speaking of the mythical creatures your own humanity created many years ago when superstition was mixed with religious fervor on Earth. Honor, when you chose life over death the only way you could be saved was for me to infuse my life essence into your body. I am not from Earth, although I was there for many years in the past, and I am well-acquainted with the culture of those ignorant days. I have made you like my own race, a being nourished by protein. Not a monster, neither revenant nor a walking corpse. Use the reasonable brain I know you have and you will realize that I am telling you the truth."

Again he stood motionless, watching me as I took a deep, calming breath and tried to make my brain think. His blood lay on my tongue invitingly; actually, I wanted more of it. Raising my face toward his, I replied honestly, "This is difficult for me to absorb, Drakyn. Yes, I know that I chose life when you offered it, as I was dying after that crash, and I really have no business complaining how you saved me. However, I am still frightened. Not of you—how can I fear someone who is so good to me? Damn! I feel like an inexperienced adolescent, unable to put my thoughts into the right words…"

"Take your time. What concerns you?" he asked patiently.

"I-I feel different. Stronger, and… Drakyn, am I still at all human?" My voice cracked slightly with worry.

"Of course," he replied. "However, you have been enhanced and made so much more than you were. As you sensed, you are stronger. Honor, you have offered me anything and everything. What I need now from you is your complete trust, and no less than that." He offered a hand. "Understanding will follow, I assure you."

Staring at him in that moment, it struck me that Drakyn seemed to be a creature utterly alone. The inhabitants of this place thought of him as a monster, and yet he had treated me with total kindness and gentleness. He was making it clear that the choice was my own. I chose to continue trusting him. Taking a deep, shuddering breath, I extended my own hand toward the big man. Unexpectedly, tears flooded my eyes and I slipped into his embrace, whispering, "Help me with this, please…!"

After assuring me again that he would do so, he then suggested that we go and enjoy the meal that had been prepared for us. He insisted firmly that I would be able to concentrate on our conversation better after consuming protein. He led me through a dark hallway and then down a massive, carved staircase to a dining room one floor below. The room was large enough to be called a ballroom, but the giant table before the fireplace was set for only two places, and incredible amounts of roasted meats were piled high upon it.

I sat beside him at that table and was relieved to find that this strange hunger was easily sated by reasonable amounts of meat, and that my thirst responded to water and the odd colorless wine that Drakyn favored. There were no servants visible during the entire meal and I began to wonder if we were the only people present in the castle. However, as we rose from the table a blue-skinned Andree appeared from behind a tapestry. He eyed Drakyn questioningly even as he greeted him reverently.

Drakyn gestured him closer and said to me, "Honor, this is Pried ker D'at. He is my Port Master, and he controls the business transacted there. Pried, this is my Lady, Honor."

I could not help but blink at the rather royal-sounding appellation he had added to my name, but Drakyn was so serious at the moment that I held my tongue, not wanting to give anyone the wrong impression. The high-voiced Andree greeted me with grave courtesy but his pale blue eyes were puzzled and curious as he regarded me. I wondered what, if anything, Drakyn had told him about me. I also wondered if I was just one of many female visitors who came and stayed here with Drakyn, only to be sent away later. When I glanced again at Drakyn in the next moment, and saw the warmth of his eyes as he looked back at me, I discarded my doubts as unworthy.

Drakyn walked with me through the massive castle a little later, introducing me to several other resident servants who appeared almost magically when Drakyn called for them. There were also more of his port employees, including the dark-gray felinoid called Tarquin, who was his Security Chief. I liked the giant cat-man immediately, even though I sensed he was confused and cautious about me. I resolved to get to know him better in the future. Drakyn and I eventually came to a suite of three large rooms, located two levels down from where I had awakened. Showing me inside, I realized that they had been prepared specifically for my use. They were appointed with absolutely beautiful reddish wood furniture, carved with strange figures of birds, animals, and flowers. There was a sitting room, a bedroom and a bathroom dominated by a bathing pool that appeared to have been fashioned from a massive piece of clear crystal. The suite reminded me of childhood fairy tales, and I appreciated the care that had been taken in its preparation.

In the sitting room, Drakyn and I talked long and seriously through the remainder of that day and well into the night, with Drakyn describing to me how massively and yet how little I had been transformed.

The most obvious change was dietary. I could consume only protein-rich foods, mostly meats of any kind. Blood drinking was optional and Drakyn assured me that there was no reason for me to do so if I was not inclined. He admitted that he did so mostly when he was in the furious throes of his own terrible temper. Physical strength was enhanced among our kind, and he told me that I was now probably stronger than four normal human males. This would give me a physical advantage over most known races both within and outside of the Fleet. Anger enhanced that strength, so that volatile emotion needed to be controlled or avoided altogether, if possible. However, blood drinking between the two of us was always possible, and could be particularly pleasurable and satisfying during sexual sharing. The manner in which he spoke of the dangers of anger made me realize that this was probably his greatest personal challenge. Obviously, when he unleashed his own temper great damage resulted. This explained why he kept himself apart, even from the others who inhabited this fortress with him. He did so to protect them from him.

Further, Drakyn taught me that I was now immune to all known diseases, that I would learn to heal my body using my strength of will, and that my aging process was now slowed to a virtual standstill. He estimated that we aged physically about one week for each standard year of life, resulting in near-immortality when compared to other sentient life forms. Only complete starvation from protein food sources could throw off the non-aging process. He also informed me that the changeover to his life form had completely disrupted my female reproductive systems, thus I would be totally unable to conceive a child for another solar year. By the end of that year I would again be able to assert control over my own cycles, as was second nature to any female serving in the Fleet where unplanned pregnancies were almost nonexistent. When I cautiously asked Drakyn if he was going to expect me to produce a child for him, he merely smiled and shook his head negatively. That relieved me of some anxiety.

It was obvious that I needed time to grow accustomed to this new version of life I was experiencing, and I would need to remain close to Drakyn as I did so. My instincts had always been very good about people and they told me that this handsome, possessive alien male was being very honest with me.

Late in the night, when I had twice covered my mouth to hide a yawn, Drakyn rose and kissed my hand saying, "I sleep very little myself, but you still need sleep, little one. I must remind myself of your present physical limitations."

He turned as if to move away, but I wrapped my hand around his big one and got up as well.

"Stay with me?" I requested softly.

He looked down at me and smiled in his serious manner. "Of course I shall if you wish it," he replied, "Until you sleep, Honor."

Moving toward the open bedroom doorway, I grinned up at him and whispered, "But I don't want to sleep. Not just yet…"

He then demonstrated his delight in fully obliging my wishes.

During the next few weeks I learned even more about Drakyn. He was the absolute ruler of Viste, and he also dominated the trade and economy of most of the sector of space in which his planet existed. This said much about the power he wielded; especially when one considered how close Viste was located to the Wolfen Empire. I also learned that he was greatly feared by many, and that he had been spoken of much more harshly than the stories quoted in this history. I had no doubt that he deserved most of what was said of him. Even so, some situations had been exaggerated or misunderstood. For example, I was not hypnotized, drugged, or dazzled by him. However, when I gave myself to him, even that first time, it was through an instinctual trust rather than a rational decision. The reasoning side of me still respected his power. I was certain that he never meant me any harm.

As mentioned previously, Drakyn was humanoid but he didn't originate from Earth or any of its settlements on other planets. He told me that he had lived on Earth many, many years before space travel had been developed there, and that he left the planet seeking solitude. He gave few details. Viste suited his needs, and he made the planet into a haven for any and all ships that would obey the rules and pay the fees. He had ways of dealing with those who threatened his control or tried to oppose him. Even Wolfen warriors came to hold him in a certain degree of awe because of his—pardon the expression—bloodthirsty and ruthless ways.

The advances of civilization toward a technological society drove Drakyn away from Earth. He knew that if he remained he would eventually attract those who would want his kind of power, or to wage war upon him for superstitious reasons. He enjoyed anonymity, and visitors to Viste soon learned that he disliked having his name spoken away from the planet. It became common practice to simply refer to him as the "Lord of Viste."

Drakyn's imperceptible aging process caused those who knew him for any length of time to believe he was beyond death. The old Earth term for his type of creature was *vampire*. Like most superstitions, the associated beliefs offered a very incorrect summary. Drakyn was born a protein consumer, while I was changed, by the infusion of his life energy, into much the same kind of being. However, there was no aversion to sunlight, no shape changing, no death-like sleep, or coffins. My attraction to and affection for this powerful, solitary male did not blind me to my surroundings, and I remained essentially the same woman I had always been.

Still requiring more rest than Drakyn, I often retired to my suite of rooms fairly early in the evenings simply because exhaustion compelled me to do so. About two months after beginning my new life on Viste, I was awakened abruptly in my bed one night. Lying there in the firelight, I stared at the ceiling wondering if Drakyn was about to come in and join me. When it became plain that I was no longer sleepy, I got up and went to the big windows on the side of the castle that overlooked the courtyard. There were torches lit down below, and they surrounded a shuttle ship that I had never before seen. Curious about visitors, I slipped a long blue fur robe over my nightgown and went out into the frigid hall. It was early spring on Viste just then, and the corridors were never heated. I later learned how to be less sensitive to the cold, but that night I remember how chilly it was, making me shiver slightly.

Light shone at the end of the hall, coming up from a large chamber one level below. I went and stood silently on the darkened balcony overlooking that area and saw Drakyn seated there. Looking like a splendid king, he sat in a huge, carved chair at the head of the long dining table. One muscular, leather-clad leg was cast over the arm of the chair and his attention was upon his six port agents who flanked either side of the table. The remains of a meal was spread out before them, with quite an amazing assortment of foods suited to the needs of Vistens, Andree, Coryan, and the felinoid race called Malkin.

My attention was drawn to the arched doorway where a pair of pirates, one Coryan and one Andree, stood looking as if they were awaiting an audience. A large basket and a manacled young female Coryan stood behind them. I could not see the details very well from my vantage point, but it was obvious to me that the girl was terrified of Drakyn. Her eyes were riveted on him without any of the usual Coryan female's sexual confidence.

The Coryan pirate was saying, "...for your table. And, for other appetites, this female slave..."

At these words, the girl gave a start and began to speak in her native Coryan in a tone close to a shriek, but her words were cut off abruptly when the pirate turned and struck her full in the face.

"Stop! Enough!" Drakyn's voice cut through the air, halting the second blow the pirate intended. In a pleasant but danger-loaded tone Drakyn said, "You have given the slave to me. You may no longer touch her." He nodded toward the door and his agents rose at once and moved toward it, ushering the two pirates out of the hall with them.

Drakyn sat where he was, his eyes still on the girl. She stared back like a trapped wild creature. The muscles in her throat contracted as she swallowed with difficulty.

"No!" The girl suddenly shouted in Standard. She turned desperately and bolted for the tall, unglazed window to her right. She was very close to the open window.

Drakyn was out of his chair and caught her before she could throw herself out. The girl's scream sounded and was echoed by my own a moment later.

I was already running down the stairs myself, but I hesitated slightly to catch my balance when I tripped over my fur robe. In that same moment I saw Pried ker D'at re-enter the hall.

Holding the terrified girl with one arm around her slim waist, Drakyn cast a dark glance up at me as if to ascertain that I was not in any danger.

I glared back at him and dropped the blue robe from my shoulders, kicking at it in irritation. My filmy bed gown was enough at the moment.

Drakyn ignored me just then, and turned his face down toward the girl as he said, "Child, be calm. No harm will come to you. Tell me, what planet is your home?"

Sobbing still, the girl managed to reply, "Renazz, in the Wolfen sector. Please, don't hurt me!" Then her voice failed.

Drakyn's hand forced her face up to meet his compelling gaze and her sobbing abruptly stopped. He touched the girl's forehead with two fingers then and said quietly, "You shall NOT be harmed in any way. I give my word, and no one disobeys me here. See there, my own *under clad* lady comes to your aid as well!" This last sentence was mocking me a bit as I came closer, ready to throw myself at Drakyn if necessary.

Then, to the girl, but to me as well, Drakyn went on, "The fools who brought you here assumed I would kill you for your blood. Such is not my way. Your mind tells me that you were abducted from your home planet during a raid upon your settlement. You shall be returned there—quietly. Go now with Pried ker D'at, my agent. Not all Andree are pirates. Will you trust me?"

Looking dazed, the girl silently nodded. Drakyn released her and she turned toward Pried who now offered her a slim, blue hand. He took her to the side door leading under the staircase. Pried moved as if to pick up the big basket and then stopped abruptly. He raised his gaze to Drakyn questioningly.

"What is it?" Drakyn asked. He had begun to turn toward me, but now looked back at Pried.

"This is not meat, Lord Drakyn," Pried stated, frowning a bit. "Sentient species."

I moved toward the basket before Drakyn did, but he was close behind me. In the basket lay two infant felinoids—but not Malkin, for there were no extended fangs evident like those of Tarquin and others of his species.

Drakyn commented, "Yes, definitely sentient. A male and a female infant." Turning back to the young woman he then asked, "Girl, what do you know of these?"

"My name is Rhee," the girl said, apparently feeling safe enough to sound sulky. "I never saw them before tonight."

Impulsively, I reached to touch one of the infants. Both appeared to me quite like Terran house cats, but then my touch to the nearest one's paw made the sleeping infant extend finger-like appendages tipped with delicately transparent claws. She was very young, a soft buff color with darker brown markings on her face, paws, and tail. Her brother was bluish gray.

"Tarquin's mate will care for them," Pried suggested, "Malkin females are unintelligent, but always gentle and will accept the young of any species."

Drakyn indicated his agreement, adding, "Warn Tarquin that these infants belong to me. I will hold him responsible for their health."

Pried took the girl and the infants out of the hall.

I held myself back from asking to care for the kittens myself; I knew they would do much better in the care of another felinoid. Sighing, I turned and headed upstairs to my rooms, picking up the fallen robe on my way. I did not even glance back at Drakyn, not knowing what to say. Even less likely to sleep than previously, I went to the windows that overlooked the cliff side of the castle and stood looking down at the moonlit valley below. A deer-like creature ran across a clearing, head high, graceful. Free. I was shivering despite the fire. I heard Drakyn enter, but did not turn to look at him yet. He walked behind me and put his arms around me, kissing the side of my throat possessively. I laughed softly at my own thoughts.

"You are amused, Honor?"

"I live in interesting times," I replied, smiling to myself at the words of the ancient curse. "Will you truly return Rhee to her home?"

"No," he replied. "Pried is draining her blood for my breakfast as we speak." When I gasped and turned as if to face him, he tightened his arms and kissed the top of my head. "A jest, Honor! When it is practical, she will be put aboard a trusted ship and taken home. You may see her to be certain she is safe any time you wish. . . . You ran to her aid tonight. You expected me to harm her."

Shaking my head, I replied, "I didn't know. You are unpredictable, Drakyn. I can't be certain of anything yet. I feel violence in you—sometimes it's even like a hunger—for violence sake alone rather than for blood or meat. I feel so different myself! I am a duty-bound member of the Fleet. I know where I should be. I ought to be plotting and planning ways to get away from here, from you, and back to my duty. Maybe I just enjoy being your latest favorite..."

"Favorite?" he echoed, sounding surprised. "Such an archaic term from such a modern woman. Your presence here makes me realize how much I have missed the company of human women. Coryan females are reputed to be the most desirable females in the universe. In certain ways they are. Andree females are more alien, but they also have their charms. Even some Wolfen women are lovely in their raw animalistic sexuality. But you, Honor, remind me of my own race. Humans are the most delightful and challenging of all sentient beings—in many ways like my own people. No wonder your Fleet is so powerful. I shall regret it when I am compelled to let you go your own way."

Turning around to face him fully, I said, "You haven't mentioned that to me before. What is the term of my gentle servitude with you?"

His expression became cold. I had insulted him. His hands on my arms tightened painfully for a moment before he deliberately relaxed the grip. "You enjoy trying to antagonize me, don't you? Or is it all men? You claim to enjoy my company. What do YOU wish?"

Finding it difficult to meet his eyes just then, I kept my gaze directed to the pulse-point in his throat. "I don't exactly know yet, Drakyn. Things feel so new to me with you! I am content just now to hide here in your big shadow. I don't know if I can exist among my own people as a blood drinker. Maybe I'm still healing?"

Drakyn became gentle again. "Your entire way of viewing life is changing, Honor. You must learn what your new nature is to be. It has been many years since I have given another human the touch of my species. I was foolish to do so on Earth, at least as it was when I dwelt there. As a race, you humans were not ready for it. Everyone I touched with my nature was eventually destroyed by his or her own impatience and villainy. Yet you, Honor, have the intelligence and even temperament necessary to harness your powers."

A bit worried by his admission, I asked, "Drakyn, will I ever be able to return to my old life? Will what you've changed about me make me an outcast? An exile?"

His eyes seemed almost sad. "This is entirely up to your truest self. If you are inclined toward violence as a rule, then this will be enhanced and magnified as it is in me. During the many years of my life, I have learned to keep myself apart to control this tendency, to serve penance for my past mistakes. You have only the smallest spark of me within you, Honor. If you are wise, it will not overtake what you *are* and wish to be. You will simply have certain talents and needs that will be unlike others of your birth race. It will be for your Fleet to be tolerant and wise about you."

Leaning against his broad chest, I murmured, "For now, I am content to stay here with you."

His hand smoothed my hair as he said, "Honor, there are those with whom I regularly deal who are sworn enemies of your Fleet and therefore your enemies. Most of them fear the Fleet's laws. Your background must be kept a strict secret between you and me for that reason. I do not want the Fleet to have any cause to come here."

"I understand," I said quickly, "I don't want anyone else to find out either. But I cannot and will not be kept locked in this castle like some courtesan of yours. I need freedom! I know there are other women here..."

"NONE are like you!" Drakyn assured me vehemently. "Most feel safe here, freed from slavers or worse. They remain only until I contrive a manner to return them to their homes, like young Rhee. And you need not stay in the castle if you wish to go out. Word of your survival and my interest in you has already reached the port city. You are safe here; no one would dare touch you."

"Drakyn, I'm not about to play queen or countess either..."

"No," he interrupted, wrapping me in his cloak as he held me close to him. After a silent moment, he surprised me by saying, "You have a talent for small ships. Designing and building them interests you. Use your talent, Honor. Many in the port would be eager for your skills. The little craft you crashed was not irreparably damaged. It is berthed in the port. Perhaps you should address its repair."

I laughed and replied, "I owe you a ship, at least!"

Drakyn's sensuous lips went to my throat; I closed my eyes and enjoyed it.

Chapter 6

Unfettered

DRAKYN had Honor escorted by Tarquin down to the main port in Viste City the first time she traveled there. In preparation, the big felinoid appeared at the designated time on the ground level of the castle where surface shuttles were parked, the hair at the back of his head slightly fluffed in concern.

Lord Drakyn's woman was already there, walking around the surface shuttle in the manner of one curious about its mechanisms. Hearing him approach, she turned at once and flashed a smile at him, saying, "Good morning, Tarquin. Thank you for agreeing to take me to the port today. Drakyn seems to believe that I still need protection, so I apologize if I am taking you away from your work."

"My work is to serve Lord Drakyn's wishes," Tarquin neutrally replied, unable to keep himself from examining the female's pleasing features. She was even smaller than he recalled, but she moved with a confidence that suggested she was far more powerful than one might assume. Word had already spread that she was a protein consumer in the manner of Lord Drakyn. People speculated that this might have been why Drakyn chose to keep her alive, and why he took such care to help the female recover from her injuries.

Pleasantly continuing, Honor inquired, "Did Drakyn tell you

where I want to go in the port?"

Tarquin slid open the portal on the shuttle and indicated that the female should precede him inside. "You wish to inspect the ship that you crashed when you arrived on Viste. The Lord has also arranged for a ship's engineer to meet you there."

Honor went up the two steps into the shuttle, but paused to look directly into the felinoid's eyes, asking, "How are the two kittens? Do you think they'll be all right?"

"Kittens?" Tarquin puzzled over the word, then realized what she meant and was a bit startled by her concern for the castoff felinoid children.

"You know, the two felinoid infants you took to your wife last night," Honor elaborated, unsure if he had understood her question. "You did do that, didn't you?" She finally asked, and frowned a bit.

Pulling himself up straight, Tarquin turned and towered over the tiny female. He fully wanted to intimidate her because she was now very close to insulting him by doubting his word. "The children are thriving, and they shall continue to do so, my Lady. If you wish, I will have my mate bring them to you some time."

"Thank you!" Honor said enthusiastically. She touched his muscular arm for a moment. "I'd love to see them! I know Drakyn has a way of being unapproachable, but if those children need anything special that is difficult to get, please let me know! I think I can persuade him to obtain whatever it is." Then she turned and slipped into one of the passenger seats.

Tarquin stared at her a moment longer, startled by her sincere-sounding offer, and equally baffled by the energetic enthusiasm this female exuded. She seemed to have a kind heart, yet he suspected that she could also be a force to be seriously reckoned with should her energies be focused against anyone she considered an enemy. Perhaps she was a better match for the Lord than he had originally thought. The female became rather quiet as he started the land vehicle and drove the short distance to Viste City. From the castle, they traveled down winding roads through heavy forest. Tarquin was busy guiding the vehicle and speaking over a voicelink to the port, but he was aware that Drakyn's Lady was interested in watching how he drove. When they reached and parked in the port area, Tarquin escorted her the short distance to the berth where the wrecked shuttle now reposed in pieces.

Honor thanked Tarquin again for bringing her here, but her eyes were now riveted on the damaged ship. One wing was completely pulled free from the structure. Insulation and wires trailed from the broken pieces. Computer boards lay strewn about the wreck like scattered coins. Tarquin had moved a few steps away, but could not resist turning back to look at the female once more. She walked slowly around the wreck, a tight little smile on her lips as she ducked under a fallen strut and climbed inside. He finally moved away, shaking his head.

Inside the ship, Honor blinked down at the pilot's chair. A large portion of metal from the deck had been pushed upward during the crash, pinning the seat backward at an awkward angle. Dark, old blood stained the leather seat and a bit of black cloth was stuck to it. Feeling somewhat sick as she relived her memories of the crash, Honor staggered slightly as she moved back to the exit. Something crunched under her feet and she glanced down to see blue and silver crystals from the gown she had been wearing during her escape attempt. Moving quickly outside, she leaned against the side of the ship to collect her feelings. Breathing deeply and slowly, she reminded herself that she was healed now. Even so, her chest and legs ached with the memory of those injuries and she struggled to regain some sense of calm, wondering vaguely if Drakyn had sent her here intending for her to face this memory.

"You are ill?" a thickly accented voice inquired from somewhere nearby, making Honor jump like a startled cat. Opening her eyes, she regarded a large and burly alien that could only barely be classified as humanoid—meaning simply that he had two legs, two arms, and one head. His features were somewhat obscured by thick, brown-gray fur and his snout was porcine. It was impossible to read any kind of emotion but aggression in his marble-black eyes. Again, he demanded, "You are ill?"

"No..," she replied, trying to smile at him. "I was..." She did not know how to explain herself, but then she wondered why she was trying to do so.

It was unnecessary to say more just then, because the big alien huffed impatiently and turned his gaze onto the ship behind her. He swung to face her again and demanded, "You are the human female called 'Honor,' no? . . . Pried ker D'at jokes with me!"

Staring at the creature, she said, "I don't understand."

Thumping his chest with a hand that boasted four fingers and a thumb, each topped with a tiny hoof, the alien said belligerently, "I am a top mechanic and engineer! The best in all port! The Andree Pried ker D'at came to me and hired me to help the human woman rebuild a two-being ship! I find her weeping and a twisted hunk of broken metal at her back! Impossible! Impossible!"

Pulling her wits together, Honor surveyed his not-too-clean coveralls and realized who and what he was. Taking the offensive, she began, "Well, I plan to rebuild this ship. If it is beyond your skills, then that is your problem, sir!" With that she moved away from him, around to where the tail section should have been located.

As she fully expected, the alien lumbered after her, shouting, "Beyond MY skills! You know nothing of me! I could rebuild this tiny ship in a week if I wished!"

Grinning to herself, Honor resisted the temptation to make him bet on that but instead she demanded, "What is your name?"

That made him pause in the tirade he was building. "I am Gall of Tredar, and no other name is necessary. My expertise is known the galaxy over!"

"Fine," Honor said, "My name is Honor, of Earth. If Pried hired you, I guess I'm stuck with you, for now. I am here to work on this ship, Gall of Tredar. You can stand there shouting, but I'm not listening." She grabbed a stool and stepped onto it so that she could inspect the damage done where the rear thrusters had been torn away.

By the end of the afternoon Honor had compiled a long list of equipment and parts she was going to need to work on the ship. Gall and Honor had also discovered that they both knew what they were talking about when it came to the mechanics of the ship, and on that basis they would be able to work together. Gall irritated Honor at first, but she eventually came to be amused by his constant mutterings and boasts and complaints. Surprisingly, the one thing he never challenged her on was her skills. He also proved to be very knowledgeable about how Port Viste actually functioned, and he was invaluable in finding the equipment and computers they needed to do their work.

Honor was startled a few hours later when she climbed out of the ship and found herself facing a small crowd of port workers, or else visitors of some sort. They stood far enough away that she could not consider them any kind of threat, but she was unnerved somewhat by their intense curiosity. She flinched slightly when Gall spoke from directly behind her, saying, "The word has spread that Drakyn's Woman is here. Ignore them. They will not dare to approach you."

Pushing the hair out of her eyes, Honor glanced at the porcine mechanic, smiled, and then asked, "Do they expect me to show my fangs and snarl at them?"

"*I've* seen no fangs," Gall rumbled, unnecessarily polishing a piece of metal with a cloth.

Realizing he was asking a question indirectly, Honor stated gently, "Yes, I do have them, Gall. I am a blood drinker, like Lord Drakyn. Even Drakyn's fangs don't show all the time, you know."

When she glanced at his face, Honor was certain that he was about to ask her a direct question, but then his eyes went back toward the crowd. "They're scattering now. Ah, see. Pried is approaching us."

The Andree Port Master approached them soundlessly, seeming to glide over the floor in his long, blue robes. His light blue eyes were intent upon Honor. "My Lady Honor, are you satisfied with Gall of Tredar's skills? Do you require more or other assistance?"

"Gall of Tredar is a master mechanic," Honor replied somewhat formally. "I am certain we shall work together well on this project, Pried. Thank you for asking." She picked up her note pad and looked at it again, expecting the Andree to move away.

"My Lady Honor," Pried said somewhat hesitantly, "The Lord of Viste has sent me to escort you back to the castle now. You will come with me."

Honor waited two heartbeats before turning to face him. She did not like the sound of command behind the words. "No, I don't think so. We're in the midst of something here. I'll go back later." Then, turning around she asked, "Gall, can you give me a ride to the castle when we're done for the day?"

The mechanic appeared slightly uncomfortable. "Honor," he

began, "If the Lord of Viste has sent for you, it is best that you immediately accompany Pried ker D'at…"

Pushing down a flare of temper, Honor shook her head and interrupted him. "No. I'm not a servant who will run to his summons whenever Drakyn calls for me. He knows that. Pried, if he needs to see me, tell Drakyn he can come here himself. I'll be right here." Then she went back inside the ship and ignored Pried even when he called her name twice.

Then Gall came inside the ship and rumbled, "Why do you hate Pried ker D'at? He is a harmless creature. Has he offended you?"

"Hate him?" Honor echoed, "Don't be silly…"

Nodding toward the portal, Gall said, "It may be that I overstep myself with you, Honor, but you seem a reasonable female. Surely you know that the Lord of Viste is regarded with fear, and that he is to be obeyed! Pried is likely to be killed when he delivers your reply to the Lord's summons."

"No, he won't—I'm just letting Drakyn know that I'm not going to run to his beck and call and… Oh… God! Gall, I'll see you in the morning! Bye!" Honor dropped her keypad and jumped out of the ship.

Pried ker D'at was halfway across the hangars, walking steadily, but with his head hanging in the manner of one doomed to a terrible fate.

Honor called his name and sprinted across the hangar after him before he heard her. She called to him again as she approached and then impulsively caught his arm, slipping hers through his and saying, "Oh Pried, I apologize! I forgot how Drakyn is with people who give him answers he doesn't want to hear! Forgive me, please? I'll return with you right now!"

Stopping, the Andree bowed slightly to her and stated, "You are kind lady, but I must not force you to accompany me against your will. As you pointed out, you are NOT a slave!"

"What I am is thoughtless and selfish. This lifestyle is still a new experience for me. Again I apologize to you," Honor countered, peripherally aware that they were standing in the middle of the crowd of onlookers at that moment. All were avidly listening to the conversation between them. "Where's your transport, Pried?"

Honor: Drakyn's Lady

With another slight bow, the Andree indicated a shuttle directly ahead of them.

"Let's go, then," Honor said simply.

During the short flight back to the castle, Honor made a point of asking Pried ker D'at about himself, learning that he had a wife and five children also residing within the castle complex. By the time they reached the shuttle berth, Honor was certain that the Andree was much more comfortable in her company.

Honor went up to her suite of rooms and as she was about to enter, an Andree servant cautiously approached and informed her that the Lord of Viste awaited her in the dining hall. She thanked him for the information, asked him to tell Drakyn that she had received the summons, and then went into her rooms. She shut the door and locked it securely. Then she went in and took a hot shower to rid herself of the grime she had accumulated climbing around the wrecked ship all day. However, the warm shower did not cool her mood.

She was toweling herself after the shower when she heard knocking on her door. Honor ignored it. She shrugged into a long, warm robe and sat down near the fire in the sitting room to comb the snarls out of her long hair. Smiling, she wondered how long it would take Drakyn to come up here after her. The thought had barely formed in her mind when a much louder knock sounded at her outer door, and Drakyn called her name. The door trembled in its frame as he pounded on it.

She got up and approached the door calling, "Go away, Drakyn. I don't want to see you."

"Honor, what is this about?" he demanded, sounding both bewildered and angry. "Open this door immediately!"

Taking a deep breath, she stood where she was, staring silently at the wooden portal and bracing herself.

"HONOR!" Drakyn's voice boomed both verbally and inside her mind, his tone was one of building anger. In her mind's eye she could *see* his hand upon the metal door latch, bending it, about to break the device.

Shaking her head, Honor went to the door and unlatched it scant moments before he acted. She opened it but stood in the doorway, hands on her hips staring up at the big male. "That's how you handle everything, isn't it?" she demanded quietly,

"With force!"

Scowling in irritation, Drakyn stepped toward her but she did not retreat at all, even when he was close enough to bite her. "What is wrong with you tonight, woman?" His blood teeth were visible in his mouth.

"You," she replied seriously. "Drakyn, I know I'm really just your—your prisoner, even though you say otherwise! Well, if I'm to be a prisoner, don't lie to me about it! Keep me locked up in here. But I'll be damned if this 'inmate' will make you welcome when you come to her cell!"

Drakyn reached down and caught her waist in both hands, effortlessly lifting her from her feet and stepping into the chamber. Then he kicked the heavy door shut behind him.

"Put me down," Honor hissed at him, though not even struggling.

He complied, honestly mystified by her strange change in attitude. "Explain what this is about, Honor, while I am still controlling my anger."

"You're so kind to resist your famous temper!" Honor sneered at him, pushing free of his big hands. She took three steps toward the fireplace and then turned to face him again. "This is about your dictatorship around here! Your people, even a loyal partner like Pried, are all terrified of you and that temper of yours! They fully expect you to tear them limb from limb if they are ever compelled to deliver negative information to you! I wasn't ready to come back from the port yet today when Pried arrived, but I could see Pried's genuine fear of your reaction if he was forced to return without me! That is horrible, Drakyn! If I am to have freedom, then it must be real freedom, not restricted by the fears you bring out in other people! Do you understand what I'm saying?"

Drakyn stared at the tiny woman who dared to defy him, and dared to tell him the truth about himself as no one had done for literally centuries. On one level he felt the compulsion born of habit to step forward and teach her to obey, using fear to dominate and break the independent will she demonstrated. He was accustomed to obedience, to unquestioning loyalty, and even reverence. He actually took two steps toward Honor with his hand outstretched to take hold of her, but then he realized that her independence and strong spirit was exactly what enthralled him about the woman. He did not want another servant, or even another whore to satisfy his physical desires. What he wanted was an equal, a mate who would challenge and fulfill his soul as well as his body's needs.

"Strangely, yes, I do understand," he said at last, dropping his hand to his side. Then he turned away from her and put a hand onto the fireplace mantle, staring into the flames for a moment before continuing. "Little one," he said, "I have much to learn from you. Plainly, I must adjust my manners with everyone here to assure your freedom of movement on Viste. I will speak with Pried and Tarquin, and try to explain how different things must be between them and you."

Honor said nothing, but merely continued to look at him until he frowned deeply.

"You don't believe me?" he then asked. "I give you my solemn word, Honor! Now, will you kindly forgive my thoughtlessness today, and join me for a meal?"

Finally she smiled at the big male, loving the softened expression in his eyes, and the way he moved his head. She stepped closer to him and put her hand up against his muscular chest, slipping it under the fabric of his tunic. Then he embraced her, holding her there without words for a long moment.

Honor knew he would keep his word to her, and she was unable to resist the impulse to move her hand over his chest, feeling the muscles there. His heartbeat increased under her fingertips and she leaned her head against him, whispering, "Do you think we could have that meal brought up here a little bit later?" Her other hand unbuckled Drakyn's thick leather belt.

"That," Drakyn whispered into her hair, "can easily be arranged, little one." Then he gasped in surprised pleasure at what her hands and mouth began doing to him.

Drakyn left Honor late that night, yet Honor was still far from able to sleep. She knew Drakyn himself had little need for sleep and left only so she could rest. Within moments of his silent departure from her rooms she sat up and leaned back against the head of the bed, her brain reviewing what she wanted to do with the wrecked ship. Thinking about the work made her feel more like herself than she had in weeks.

The next morning Drakyn himself led her down to the busy

castle shuttle berths and escorted her to a surface vehicle quite like the one Tarquin had driven to the port the previous day. "This one is yours to use," he informed her in his solemn manner. "I have spoken with my people, and they understand that you are not to be hindered in your movements. You can inform Pried ker D'at if you require anything for your building project. Does this please you?"

"More than you know!" Honor replied happily. She threw herself against him so that he automatically embraced her, and then she jumped up slightly so that she could kiss his mouth. "Thank you, sweetie! I'll see you…" she said with a smile as she started to turn.

However, Drakyn's arm tightened firmly around her waist for a moment, interrupting her words and movement. Then he stared down into her face intently and whispered, "You are…amazing, Honor."

Grinning, she replied, "No more than you are, Lord Drakyn. See you later!"

Then he released her and watched the little female jog over to the vehicle and climb inside. Drakyn had to restrain himself from following her, and from insisting upon accompanying her. He wished to spend his entire day just being close to her. However, it was plain that she needed to pursue her own interests in her own way. At such moments he felt as if he was trying to hold a living flame in his hands, and he knew such an effort was useless. Sighing, he made himself turn and walk away, unwilling to stand and watch her departure like a lovesick fool.

When he turned, Drakyn realized that several of his staff had witnessed the embrace and their conversation. He resisted the urge to snarl at them, to remind them he was still the Lord of Viste. He was further startled when a ginger-colored felinoid approached him a bit shyly and spoke up, saying, "My Lord, thank you for sending the infants to our home. They have made both Tarquin and me very happy."

It took Drakyn a moment to realize that this was Cinna, Tarquin's mate. He had never heard her speak before. Keeping his tone gentle, Drakyn said, "I am pleased to hear this, Cinna. Do not hesitate to ask for anything you require for their care." He nodded politely to her bow and then moved away from the shuttle area, aware of the many sets of surprised eyes watching him.

Drakyn was distracted all morning, despite the amount of work he had intended to complete in his office. Among others, there were messages from a Wolfen captain and a Coryan pirate captain, both wishing to meet with him separately to mediate a dispute. Drakyn had intended to deal with the issue decisively that morning, but he could not seem to focus his full attention on anything but how Honor made him actually FEEL. It had been so long, he wished to savor his recollection of those emotions again. He also searched his long memory to discover just why he had suppressed emotional attachment to anyone or anything, but he found no answers, only more determination to make Honor the central focus in his life. He knew he was making himself vulnerable in doing this, but he was unable to stop.

Yes, he was unwise. He was driven. He was in love with her.

Chapter 7

Loss

NOW that I had a project on which to focus my full attention and skills, I began to feel much more comfortable in my new lifestyle and surroundings. I spent days and weeks working with Gall on the wrecked ship. We stripped it down to her bare bones and then completely rebuilt her from the skeleton up, adding some design modifications I had in mind. Even Gall had to admit that if we succeeded according to the plans I had drawn, the finished ship would be a thing of beauty and grace as well as functioning power.

Gall and I almost lived in the docks. There were days when I worked so late that I actually fell asleep inside the ship and awakened stiff and chilled in the middle of the night, or else early the next morning. Even though he did not make it obvious, I sensed that Drakyn had people keeping an eye on me, just so he knew my location at all times. Also, after that first day down in the port, the word was out among the inhabitants that *Drakyn's Lady* was around. It became very common in those first weeks to find myself being stared at by several beings of assorted races.

Common interests can join people of any species. As I spent more and more time in the docks, I came to be accepted as part of the surroundings by the regular work crews. Other engineers, mechanics, and technicians lost much of their caution as they interacted with me and with Gall in our efforts to obtain parts or programming information. They came to realize that I spoke the same professional language they did, and we slowly became comfortable with each other and learned from each other. Much of the alien technology and craftsmanship proved invaluable to me over the years. The few times Drakyn appeared in the docking area, he never approached my project. I was grateful for this, as I suspected that if he was nearby it might damage my comfortable interactions with the men who worked around us.

Almost four weeks later, I returned from the port area late one evening and went to several rooms before at last finding Drakyn in the large gymnasium-type chamber. The Lord of Viste was stripped to the waist and working through stylistic movements with a sword. The blade somewhat resembled a broadsword, but its handle was studded with sharp-edged barbs. This exercise was something he performed often, and I loved watching him completing the movements. The expression on his face was invariably intense with concentration and effort. Further, the muscles of his shoulders, arms, and back rippled as he moved, and the skin shone slightly with perspiration. Seeing him this way almost made my mouth water.

Exhaling to clear the distraction from my brain, I spoke up, "Drakyn-sweetie, I'm taking my little ship out tomorrow morning to test it…"

He saluted an invisible opponent and then glanced at me and asked in his abrupt manner, "Will your friend Gall accompany you on this flight?"

"Actually, no," I replied cautiously, "Gall is somewhat skeptical about the design of the energy inducer I've installed, but it's just because he's never seen one working before…"

"May I accompany you, then?" he asked as he picked up a towel, wiped his face, and then reached for a goblet of the synthetic protein drink he favored. He knew I was anxious to see if my new features and modifications would work as I had planned, but I was also nervous because I had not piloted anything but my tiny ground vehicle since the crash.

I grinned happily at his offer and nodded my agreement, adding, "I promise not to give you a heart attack with my piloting, Drakyn!"

"That," he said dryly, "is unlikely."

Moving closer to him, I said, "I have a request."

"Anything, little one," he said, with his solemn smile that I was beginning to see more often, "Everything."

The smile made my heart pound. It was difficult to keep myself from touching him. "I want to learn how to use this kind of sword. I can fence reasonably well. I learned to use a rapier at the Academy. But I wish for you to teach me this style!"

His dark, dark eyes seemed slightly surprised for a moment but then he smiled a bit and turned toward the computer link on the wall, saying, "First, we must fabricate a weapon for your use..." Soon we were again engrossed with each other, finding joy through our shared hearts and souls.

***

MY trial flight went very well, despite the fact that I felt my stomach clench in nervousness the moment the bay doors rolled open and I faced blue sky again. Drakyn's calm presence beside me was enormously reassuring even though he did nothing to participate in piloting the craft that day.

The ship had been enameled a shiny blue-black color, and was not only equipped with triple deflector shields, but her power had been increased multiple times, as well. As I worked on her, I dreamed of taking her all the way back to Fleet space—even to Earth—and landing at Fleet Headquarters and surprising the hell out of old friends who undoubtedly believed I was dead. I knew I could not, but I dreamed of it. Although the ship did not perform perfectly during that first flight, she did well. Most importantly, I discovered I had not lost any of my nerve; I could still skillfully pilot a ship. Drakyn seemed quietly impressed by my work, and when I remarked that I owed him the ship because I had stolen it, he firmly disagreed.

"The ship is yours to keep, little one," he stated, "You have earned it. Now name it and keep it."

"The *Freedom*," I whispered immediately, "Thank you!"

After the most time-consuming work on the ship was done, Drakyn would at times suggest that I offer assistance or advice to one or another of the people working on other ships in port. Soon I found myself growing deeply involved with numerous other ships' problems. Gall became absolutely indispensable to me, and he seemed content to remain my partner, no matter what project we had to complete. At Drakyn's suggestion, I began berthing the *Freedom* in the same small docking area he used at the base of the mountain below the castle. There I could work alone in peace and privacy.

Gall seldom came to that docking area, preferring to remain within the port itself. I would have worked there all alone, but for the two felinoid kittens that had arrived the same night as Rhee. Tarquin and his mate Cinna had taken exceptional care of the children and they were thriving. The kittens had gone unnamed until Tarquin insisted that I should choose names for them. The beige and brown little female became known as Morgana, and the male was Merlin because his blue-gray fur reminded me of a wizard's cloak. They may have been sentient children who would one day grow into highly intelligent beings, but at approximately one year of age they were as playful and naughty as any Terran kitten I had known. They seemed oblivious to rules and correction. An exception was their father figure, Tarquin, whose fierce sounding snarl and hiss stopped them in their tracks. Then, either one or both of the children would make a point of moving up close to the big felinoid warrior with displays of innocent affection, until even Tarquin was moved to grant them a forgiving tongue swipe.

Observing such an encounter, I was hard pressed not to laugh out loud and thereby embarrass or irritate the generally gruff and dignified Tarquin. It was not unusual to observe Drakyn himself seated at his council table with his agents, deep in conversation about port or sector business, with at least one of the kittens curled asleep on his lap or else nearly crowding him out of the big chair. The children seemed unimpressed even when Drakyn raised his deeply resounding voice to shout at someone. Drakyn was amazingly patient with them, even when Merlin chose to leap onto his table during a meal, or Morgana attached her claws to the hem of his long cloak as he walked. Of course, that sort of behavior set Tarquin hissing at them until they fled to Cinna for protection—or to me, because they always received indulgence and affection from me.

Within six months Morgana and Merlin grew more independent, and at times even chose not to return to Cinna at night.

Instead they joined me in my own bed when I was alone. I became very accustomed to and fond of settling down to sleep listening to the sound of their purring, and I enjoyed the warmth of their little furry bodies curled up beside me. The only thing that would banish them from my room was Drakyn. If he came to join me, he would quietly put them out of my suite into a servant's room, or carry me away in his arms to his own quarters. On the days I spent long hours working in the private docking area, I often enjoyed the youngsters' company. I soon grew used to the sound of their scampering and thumping over, under, around, and through the piles of equipment, tools, and parts in the area. Sometimes they were even helpful, learning to identify tools by their names or descriptions and fetching them for me. Mostly to keep them out of trouble, I began finding constructive things for them to do when their play became too rowdy or accidentally destructive.

Felinoids grow and mature out of childhood somewhat faster than human children, and at a year these two spoke about as fluently as 4-5 year old humans. They also grew very good at learning languages and could switch between Andree, Standard, and Coryan with no noticeable confusion. Their intelligence and quick adaptability continually surprised and pleased me. After the first year, Merlin and Morgana suddenly doubled their height and weight within four months. They began attending classes together with other children native to Viste, taking them away from the castle for several hours a day. When they were not being instructed, both still loved to run and climb and play everywhere in and around the castle. Watching them, I often wondered if someone was searching desperately for them somewhere in the galaxy, but I knew the likelihood of finding their family was nonexistent. It had already been more than a year.

The passing of that much time disturbed me on several levels. I had been with Drakyn for more than a year myself. I had drastically changed my lifestyle and my dietary habits. I also knew, on an intellectual level, that I was no longer entirely human, but I had yet to come face to face with what I really had become. This was largely because I was protected and safe and quite insulated under Drakyn's wing on Viste.

Change is inevitable, everywhere in the universe.

No matter where they went in space, it seemed the violent Wolfen race managed to create problems for any other sentient races they encountered. Even on Viste they were troublemakers, though few remained there long enough to draw Drakyn's anger. Wolfen are very superstitious, and Drakyn's power and reputation tended to unnerve them.

One night perhaps a year and a half after I had come to Viste, Pried ker D'at came to see Drakyn as we dined. Pried announced that a Wolfen destroyer was in orbit and signaled its intention to send down a landing party to meet with Drakyn.

Looking a bit annoyed at the news, Drakyn instructed Pried to inform the Wolfen that he would find time to meet with them in the morning, at the port offices. After he had gone, Drakyn looked across the table at me and said, "Honor, I want you to keep out of sight during this Wolfen visit. These are not pirates, nor dissident independent merchants. They are officers from a military ship, and space traffic news has been carrying hints that the political situation between your Fleet and the Wolfen is deteriorating. I do not want any incidents."

"Who don't you trust? Them or me?" I wondered aloud.

"It is well known that the Wolfen military hates Terran humans, Honor. Whether or not the feeling is mutual, the very sight of you might start something more than they are already plotting."

"You're human-looking too," I pointed out, becoming a bit annoyed myself. "For all they know you're Terran human, and they deal with you, don't they?"

Drakyn stood up. "They know I am NOT Terran. Wolfen are predictably violent, Honor. I use their own superstitions to keep them at a distance from Viste. On occasion, they force me to demonstrate my temper in their presence."

Smiling somewhat smugly, I remarked, "I see. I think you don't want me to see that famous temper of yours in action more than you don't want them to see me here."

He suddenly became very serious, and his dark brows knit together in a deep frown. "Honor, this is more than just a request from me."

"Is it a command, then?" I challenged cheerfully. I was enjoying baiting him a little bit. After so much time had passed, Drakyn really did not worry me much anymore.

His incredibly strong hand pulled me around irresistibly to face him. In a whisper, he said, "I cannot command you, Honor. One-to-one physically is the only way I can try to control you. This is a polite . . . request!"

"And I shall obey you, Master!" I said very demurely, my eyes downcast in the manner of a slave girl. I believe that was as close as I ever saw Drakyn come to laughter. Instead, we just embraced without passion.

So I spent the next day in the castle, working on the *Freedom* down in the docking area. By this time it was merely a matter of fine-tuning a ship that I already considered my best accomplishment. Alone in the bay one hundred meters below the lowest level of the castle, no one from above could observe whatever occurred down there. I was lying on my back underneath the *Freedom*'s belly, checking a loose seal when my brain suddenly registered a sound that I had not heard since coming to Viste. It was the signature whine of a molecular transporter in use nearby. When I turned my head, I saw three sets of heavy boots, studded with hooked barbs—Wolfen boots. Before I could move or react in any way, a grating voice exclaimed, "What is this?" and clawed hands grasped my ankles and yanked me out from under the ship. I was hauled up to my feet by a rough hand at the throat of my shirt.

"A *human* female!" The ugly Wolfen commander (I recognized the signs of rank from Enemy Identification 101) growled in passable Standard. He confidently holstered his blaster with his free hand. He was a poor example of personal hygiene, even for a Wolfen. His skimpy beard was uncombed and stained with something yellow. "Unusual in this sector, aren't they, Krell?"

The question was obviously rhetorical, but the lesser officer quickly agreed with his commander.

"Yes, my lord Verma!" Krell replied with an ugly leer at me. "This Drakyn obviously has many such valuable whores in his so-called fortress!"

At least that one is somewhat cleaner, I thought.

Wolfen was how their race's name translated into Standard, but this race of vicious warriors was nevertheless basically humanoid in body type. I knew from my Academy studies that they had clawed hands and feet. The ridge of rough-textured hair on their heads extended down to the base of their spines terminating at the short remainder of what was once an actual tail. Their red-brown skin was stretched over an oversized skull that appeared very ugly to Terran sensibilities. Looks could be discounted as unimportant, but their uniformly aggressive and destructive actions had ensured them a place as one of the Fleet's worst enemies.

Most inhabitants of Fleet-protected space had lost one or more relatives as the result of Wolfen sneak attacks upon the outer colonies.

At this moment I made no effort to struggle or speak, though I was sending a mental shriek of warning to Drakyn. Obviously the Wolfen delegation Drakyn had agreed to meet with was a decoy so these could invade his stronghold. I had no idea if my mind could reach his, but I tried.

Verma now produced a long knife from a hip sheath. "We will leave Drakyn a surprise after we've enjoyed her." With an ugly show of badly stained teeth, he yanked me through the open double doors and into the daylight. Glancing back at Krell, he said, "Investigate that craft. She will remain alive for your turn with her."

Outside, I tried to break free, but his strong hand effortlessly knocked me flat onto my back. As I scrambled over the rough stones to get to my feet, the Wolfen suddenly howled sharply as a bundle of beige and brown fur leapt onto his back, digging sharp claws into his neck. It was Morgana, hissing unlike any sound I had ever heard from her. She drew dark purple Wolfen blood until the officer wrenched her free and roughly threw her away. Little Morgana bounced off the trunk of a tree and fell, stunned. The Wolfen then drew a blaster and fired at her before I could reach him. Morgana was instantly consumed in a flash of white flame.

I can still hear her last cry.

I was up on my feet now and I launched myself at the Wolfen, but the butcher's strength was still greater than mine. I was again knocked down. Then he pounced upon me, further forcing the air out of my lungs as I fought him. His foul breath was on my face and his claws cut through the front of my suede shirt, slashing the skin beneath it. At that moment, something snapped within my brain. A bubble of hate and outrage burst and expanded outward like a miniature star going nova. It was suddenly easy for me to tear one hand free. I reached up effortlessly, locking an arm around his neck and pulling him down toward me. He began to struggle now as if I was hurting him. Unrestrained fury all but blinded me as I jerked him down and my extended blood teeth met his scaly throat. He never even cried out as I killed him, the strange blood reminding me of spoiled meat as I drank it—all of it. When I tossed his limp form away from me, I rose and reached for his fallen knife, ignoring his blaster.

There was only a tiny scorched outline where Morgana had been.

Moving as if in a dream, I turned toward the bay doors where I could hear the other two Wolfen noisily routing through the *Freedom* and her equipment like fascinated simians. I slipped inside and kept to the shadows near the door controls. One of the two glanced up and said something softly and then stepped toward the door, chuckling. The other also laughed, but he was more interested in the *Freedom*'s interior. A moment later when the first one reached the doors, I caught him and drove the long knife deeply into his heart and then I bit his throat out of pure fury. He went down with a sigh, looking very surprised. I punched the door control, and as the heavily-shielded doors slammed down I turned to face the last Wolfen warrior.

It was the one called Krell. He came at me with smug confidence on his face, not even bothering to draw his blaster when he saw that I was alone. He brought out his own blade, shouted a word in Wolfen and ran at me like a charging bull. I moved easily, with dreamlike calm, and slashed open his arm from shoulder to elbow. He rushed at me again, trying vainly now to use his uninjured arm to reach his blaster. Again I stepped aside, but managed to sever the thick strap holding his holster in place. It clattered with the blaster to the floor.

Concerned now, he scrambled backward from me, producing what I later realized was a communications device. He shouted a single word into it and almost immediately dissolved into the molecular transporter wave as I reached for him.

Standing there in the sudden silence, I stared down at the pool of purple-black Wolfen blood where he had been. Then I turned, stumbling over the dead one as I hit the door control. My stomach truly rebelled as I staggered outside into the clean air. I knelt in the grass and was sick.

Sobbing and retching, I saw my own blood flowing from a long slash that began at the base of my throat and continued nearly to my waist. I did not realize that I had also been shrieking wordlessly until the pain in my throat made my voice fail. The thought uppermost in my mind fairly screamed out: *THIS IS NOT WHAT I WANT TO BE! NOT A KILLER! NOT A KILLER!*

I knelt there, near hysteria and horrified by my own actions. I did not hear anyone behind me until I felt the cold burn of a jagged blade as it plunged between my shoulder blades. Immobilized by pain and immediately weakened by my lifeblood exploding from the wound, I dropped face-down into the grass. For the second time I felt death reaching for me and had no idea how to fight it except by my own will. As my eyesight faded I expected life to end.

Later I awakened in a quiet, fire-lit room. I lay on my own bed, covered by furs. There was still an ache between my shoulder blades, but I could tell that it had more than half-healed already. I was not in any danger of death now. Knowing he was there, I spoke up: "Drakyn? Where are you..?"

From a large chair near the fire, his voice replied, "Here."

"I thought I was going to die."

"For you and me, death is difficult to achieve with a mere stab wound, Honor. If the cowards had been intelligent enough to cut your throat, you might have died after all. When I reached you, they had gone and you were close to shutdown, a kind of shock. Not human shock. It was much more serious. Our physicality instinctively protects us by closing down all bodily functions in order to repair the damaged area. I immediately gave you fresh blood, and this stimulated your body to repair itself quickly and efficiently. If I had been delayed longer, I would have been unable to help you to heal so quickly."

I tried to sit up, and failed. Suddenly I was crying again, sobbing like a child. I remembered what I had seen, and what I had done that day. My close brush with death was totally irrelevant to me. More than anything I wanted Drakyn to come over and hold me in his arms, comfort me, and assure me that all would be well. Instead, Drakyn stayed where he was, somehow removed emotionally from me as well as physically. After a while, when I had made an effort to stop my own sobbing, he said, "Honor, it has been nearly two years since I gave my nature to you, and you have never before faced the violence you are capable of...until today. You have killed with your strength and your teeth, and you have unleashed your greatest anger for the first time..."

"And the last!!" I declared, shakily pulling myself up on one elbow to look at him. His expression told me he was skeptical about my statement, so I burst out saying, "Drakyn, those...those animals killed Morgana! Did you know that? That child tried to help me! I had a good reason to do that to them! But I can't...I REFUSE...I will NOT become a..."

"Monster?" he finished for me with heavy irony.

I said nothing, as it was the word I had stopped myself from using.

Even in the firelight I could see him sigh and square his shoulders before he said, "I quite agree that you were justified. I dealt with the decoy landing party at the port offices today, Honor. My bloody reputation will be enhanced. Unfortunately, your attacker escaped my revenge. But the Wolfen ship responded to *my* actions by firing upon the port city and then immediately breaking orbit and running away. Four Andree ships have pursued the Wolfen ship, but I will order them to return rather than enter Wolfen space. Many people were killed in the Wolfen attack." He ran a hand over his eyes. "These people call me their protector. I also am guilty, Honor."

We were both silent for a few breaths of time, and then he spoke again, saying, "Honor, one of the first questions you asked me was what you would become here, in my company. Would your new life overtake you and change you into something else. Do you recall this?"

Drawing a deep breath, I replied, "Yes, I do. I really understand now what you told me then, Drakyn. It *is* totally up to *me* what I become, good or bad. It's up to what I *am—in my soul!*"

"Exactly," he agreed, intensely emphasizing the response. "I chose my own path of violence longer ago than you can comprehend, when it was accepted, even venerated among my race, not unlike the Wolfen. I cannot change my nature. Nor can you." He paused a moment and then added, "Honor, I know you do not wish to surrender to the violence within you. That always will be a choice available to you. Please keep in mind that you have become an extraordinarily powerful being. However, you must never fear to use your powers."

I managed to sit up, and then slowly got to my feet. He remained where he was, watching me. In a strange way I felt sorry for him, for his inability to resist his own tendencies toward violence. I could not help but smile at my own arrogance. I had just failed to do exactly that myself! Softly, I asked, "Can we do anything for Tarquin and Cinna and Merlin? And for the others who lost people today?" I tottered toward him and watched his shadowed face as he stared into the fire.

After a moment, Drakyn replied, "Pried has put resources at the disposal of those in need. Tarquin is with his family, and there is much concern about you, Honor, despite my assurances that you would recover quickly. There will be a ceremony for those lost within this hour..." He got up and drew me with him to the window facing in the direction of the city. "See, people are already assembling..."

I could see what appeared to be hundreds of flickering lights proceeding toward the Mirabai River that ran from north of the castle and along the mountain bordering the east edge of the city. The breeze was coming from that direction and I could hear voices singing a strangely haunting melody that tugged at my unruly emotions. "Should we, can we join them?" I asked, blinking back the urge for more tears.

Drakyn put his hands on my shoulders and then around my waist. He held me against his chest as he replied, "My presence would make most of them uncomfortable. But if you wish to go..."

"I'll stay with you," I decided at once, leaning back against his comforting solidity and now only slightly feeling the twinge of my wound. "What will the ceremony involve?"

"The bodies of the deceased have each been put into a separate funeral pyre, with the exception of a few Coryans whose bodies will be returned to their home planet. The pyres are along the side of the Mirabai River to the north. People will proceed to the pyre of their lost friend or relative and light it with the torches they carry. Then they will remain there until everything is consumed. The Andree will also sing mourning songs—all night, most likely. But before the sun rises, each individual who suffered a loss will light a small paper lamp from a pyre and place it afloat on the nearby river, freeing the spirit of the deceased. I recall a ceremony somewhat similar to this somewhere on Earth..." His voice continued, as he shared from his vast stores of memories.

Even though we did not attend in person, Drakyn and I stood watch all night at that window. Nearly fifty funeral pyres lit up the river banks in the distance for several hours and eventually the river itself appeared to be afire as hundreds of lanterns moved southward on its currents.

Several times I found myself in tears, remembering how bravely little Morgana had attempted to help me. I was still appalled by my own actions that day and I grew ever more determined to master that violent part of myself, despite whatever happened to me in the future.

I was thankful that Drakyn continued holding me close to him. I finally realized how upset he was, as well, when he admitted to me, "Honor, when I heard your call today, it was not because I sensed your fear or your danger or your grief for the child. I came in reply to that first mental shout warning me of interference with my property. My *property*, not with you! If you had not defended yourself as you have done..." He stopped speaking suddenly as if not trusting his voice.

I took his hand and drew it up close to my heart, saying, "Drakyn, please! I don't blame you for what happened! If you heard my warning, then you would have also heard any cry for help. I didn't cry for help, did I?"

"No, you did not." He turned me to face him, his eyes carefully searching my face. Then he said, "I have watched you carefully, Honor. Waiting. You work dutifully on the ships here, and you are invariably interested in their progress, but you always return with love—even obsession—to the little craft you rebuilt. Even the name you have given it is revealing: *Freedom*. That is what you want more than anything or anyone, and you wish to use that ship to achieve it."

"I'm not a prisoner here," I protested, a bit worried by his unusually morose attitude. "If I wanted to leave you, I would ask for my..."

"*Freedom?*" he finished for me, smiling slightly. We stared at each other in silence. "You have it, Honor. The ship and your freedom, in every way you truly wish it. No, I am not banishing you, or sending you away, but you may go away from Viste—from me—whenever you wish."

Again there was silence as I mulled over what he was telling me. At last, I ventured, "Drakyn, my feelings are very mixed about leaving Viste. But I do have a–a duty to return to the Fleet. You have been a soldier, you must understand duty."

"I do," he agreed. "And you have been healing yourself here with me, preparing yourself for the inevitability of leaving Viste. My desire is that, however far you may roam, you will also inevitably return here."

My emotions were at war that night. How could I even think of leaving this incredibly magnetic man that I knew I needed in my life? He was now a part of what made me whole. All I could find to say just then was: "I love you, Drakyn. More than you realize."

"Yes, you are probably right." His tone was sad and rueful, and it made my heart hurt for him.

Chapter 8

Discovery

LIKE a seed that is given the water and soil in which to germinate, the idea that I might be able to eventually leave Viste began to grow within my mind. My interest in perfecting the *Freedom* became more and more of an obsession for me. I began to consider how to make the craft able to withstand the stresses of a long-range flight back to Fleet-controlled space. I did not initially think that it was a good idea to attempt such a trip in my tiny ship. However, the *Freedom*'s fundamental efficiency and versatility, combined with each improvement I put into her, made me reconsider my first inclinations. My test flights became increasingly long-range excursions. I began to explore the outer edges of the space sector controlled by Drakyn's influence, and I was growing bolder and bolder.

My confidence was seriously challenged one day when I encountered a strange ship out near the border of the Collidian asteroid field. I was at the far edges of the space definitively under the protection of Drakyn's rule. There, I was testing the *Freedom*'s maneuverability and, honestly, amusing myself by weaving between the pieces of space rock. I was darting playfully in and out of gaps that were extremely dangerous to any ship, even one with the enhanced energy screens I had installed. At one point I came around the razor-sharp edges of a thirty kilometer-sized floating rock composed of heavy metal ore, when warning lights suddenly began to flash all over my control console. I acted swiftly to slow my pace and steady the ship, wondering what was setting off so many alarms. My scanning devices showed no ships anywhere in my vicinity. Were the sensors malfunctioning?

The asteroid around which I had been playing was giving me strange readings that piqued my curiosity, so I decided to find a clearing on its surface where I could put down my little ship and take some better readings. Technically, the surface of this large rock had its own gravity field, but it was so miniscule that I was not inclined to exit the *Freedom* and go for a stroll. An unexpected stumble could easily send me floating off into space. Instead, I attempted to use external tools to scoop up samples of the surface soil and rocks. However, I soon discovered that none of this material was loose enough to be easily sampled.

I had already used a cutting device to detach a large metal projection and was busy stowing it inside the *Freedom*'s belly before it occurred to me just what this asteroid might be. I spent a furious few ticks of time demanding answers from my sensors before the answer I suspected was confirmed by its readings. The surface on which the *Freedom* now rested was one large, fused metallic mass with a hollow core—it was not something that had naturally formed, it had been built… This was not an asteroid, it was a huge ship!

For a few heartbeats I sat absolutely still, with hundreds of thoughts flickering through my brain—most of them alarming enough to make me want to run away from this strange ship's surface as fast as possible. Instead, I forced myself to take deep breaths to calm down and then to try and decide which plan of action would be best. My biggest concern at the moment was the possibility that whoever had created this ship was aware of my presence upon its hull. My exterior scanning devices continued to show nothing approaching my ship, but that did not reassure me either. What kind of ship was this? How could they dare to enter the space Drakyn controlled? Could they be unaware of him, his rule on Viste, and his influence over the sector of space surrounding it? Was this ship even occupied, or was this just a giant derelict vessel in space? The readings from my scanner were confusing and told me absolutely nothing.

Sternly, I reminded myself that this was not the time to worry about such things. It was a time to take action before something happened to my relatively unprotected ship. It was also a time for me to get away and inform Drakyn of the presence of this ship. Every bit of sense I had cried out, warning that this vessel could be a danger to Drakyn, his settlement on Viste, and everyone around it. If there were occupants, I did not want to give them any more clues to my presence than I already had, so I simply disengaged the couplings that held the *Freedom* on the surface of the asteroid-ship. Then I used one of my grappling pole arms to push the *Freedom* slightly away from the surface. The extremely weak gravity field allowed my tiny ship to begin rising freely.

The moment we were away from the surface, I used short, well-aimed bursts of energy to push me further outward, just barely clearing some of the razor-sharp spines on the surface. If I had punctured the *Freedom*'s skin and lost atmosphere, my death would have been certain. This did not appeal to me much, so I was quite pleased when I judged myself to be far enough away from the surface to wake up my own helm and quietly guide the *Freedom* the hell out of there!

The day was full of still more surprises. I departed from the area of that giant asteroid ship, with one eye cautiously trained upon my scanners to be certain that the strange ship was not attempting to follow or stop me. Then, suddenly, it was gone... There was no sign, no energy echo, not one clue to indicate that the ship had ever been there at all! I blinked at the scanner, and was half inclined to turn around and see if I could again locate and follow the odd ship. Instead, however, I increased my power and hurried back toward Viste, to Drakyn!

Rather perturbed by the experience, I became somewhat incautious. I was already well within scanning range when I first saw the Wolfen ship. It was too late for me to avoid them, and all I could do was activate my weapons devices and duck into the relative shelter of another small cluster of asteroids. At least this bought me time to try to think of a way to maneuver out of their range. I did not want to be snagged with one of their energy tractors. All at once, the *Freedom*'s electrical systems began overloading without warning. Then all power failed and I was plunged into complete darkness, weapons disabled, helm unresponsive, and completely helpless before the approaching Wolfen craft!

Adrenalin helps a human body do wonderful things, but it can also completely immobilize a person when taken entirely by surprise and faced with a fearsome threat. It was several heartbeats before my alarmed brain realized that the failsafe battery backup systems had kicked in to continue supplying me with environmental support, and I could still hear voice traffic on the communications links. What shook me out of immobility was the sound of the Wolfen language and a voice, probably belonging to a commander, demanding a wide-range scan of nearby space and cursing at a subordinate as he did so. Holding my breath, I listened as the puzzled subordinate indicated his obedience.

The captain's voice then snarled, "The ship was clearly visible on our scans. Where has it gone, Vens?"

"It must still be there!" was the shaken reply, "No ship can move out of range without leaving a scannable energy trail, my lord! Perhaps it's lost power, but it's there!"

"Why can't we scan it? Increase the sensitivity!"

I was suddenly convinced that I recognized the voice I was hearing! It was Krell, the Wolfen officer whom I had driven from Viste on the day Morgana was murdered. The sound of his guttural tones still haunted my dreams—together with the sound of Morgana's voice as she was consumed by Wolfen blaster fire. More than anything in the universe, I wanted to be able to fire my weapons at this ugly ship, to wipe Krell from existence as I had already done to the other two Wolfen who had invaded Viste that day. It was just as well that my weapons were useless at the moment, as my inability to act probably saved me from being vaporized by the much bigger and stronger ship. As it was, all I could do was sit there, praying that they would not find me and wondering just why they were not able to do so!

Time seemed to crawl. I didn't dare try to fix my ship's systems, since whatever happened seemed to be cloaking my presence from the Wolfen's ship scanners. I was even afraid to move around within my ship. Some inadvertent noise might lead them close enough to me to be discovered. So, instead of taking evasive action, I sat there and cautiously monitored what conversation I could over the link. All the while, however, yet another part of my brain was working out what I would do when I felt safe enough

Honor: Drakyn's Lady

to do something. It suddenly occurred to me that the piece of the strange, asteroid ship currently within the belly of the *Freedom* probably had much to do with whatever cloaking or invisibility effect was occurring here. It was too similar to what I had experienced when leaving the asteroid ship for me to discount it as a possible factor.

Within a standard hour it was clear to me that the Wolfen ship was not going to discover the *Freedom*, despite their repeated scans of the area. I listened to Krell threaten physical atrocities upon his crew if they did not learn where my ship had gone. It got boring after a while, but I made myself sit quietly and turned my attention to how I might begin testing the metallic ore I had collected. The Wolfen finally decided with typical brutality of logic that they would saturate the area where they suspected my ship had gone (another small asteroid belt nearby) with energy weapons fire. Apparently Krell had concluded that this would probably destroy whatever was hiding among the rocks. Fortunately for me, the *Freedom* had drifted quite clear of those asteroids during the time period since losing power. Thus, I was in little danger, even from such a widespread discharge of weapons.

Finally, more than ten hours since I had encountered the Wolfen ship, the vessel concluded its scans and bombing of innocuous space rocks and moved on its way. The *Freedom* had never even been touched by collateral energy waves.

After they had disappeared from my scanners, I quietly waited another hour longer, deciding just how to proceed. I did not want to activate a distress beacon with the Wolfen ship still in the vicinity. I wondered how long I might be gone before Drakyn felt inclined to send out anyone to look for me, and reminded myself that I had more than once gone off for two or three days' time and then returned to Viste without causing undue concern from Drakyn.

Gall might get concerned before anyone else. I had specifically told him that I would only be out for the day when I left Viste that morning. However, I suspected that even Gall would hesitate to approach Drakyn personally with concerns about me without a greater passage of time. Anyway, even if someone came nearby who might help, how would they find me if I remained somehow cloaked from scanning devices?

I would need to fix this ship myself, and do it before the auxiliary battery power failed and I lost all atmospheric support. Sighing to myself, I got up and began testing systems via my console. With the exception of the comlink and display showing the battery levels, nothing seemed to be functioning. I quickly got into an environmental suit. I then used a hand crank to pop the floor panel that would open between the cabin and the cargo hold below. It was pitch dark inside the hold, but I used the torch attached to a helmet to find my way around down there.

My wrist scanner was giving me unusual radiation readings as I came down the ladder into the hold and shone my light onto the jagged metal of the sample I had taken from the asteroid ship. It was definitely some sort of metal alloy; several of the metals used in its composition were identifiable and several more were not. I looked more closely at my scanner, which was showing me other improbable numbers. Examining the area visually, I saw nearly immediately that the tip of the sample was twisted into a coil-like shape and lay in direct contact with a cable on the deck. It was suddenly obvious that there was a direct energy stream being channeled from that cable to the metal sample. The cable was slightly ruptured, probably by the sharp edges of the sample, and electrical and other energy was being bled into the alien metal object.

I went back above to find the tools I needed. When I returned below I simply rerouted energy from the damaged cable back toward an unaffected line. The moment I switched the lines, the *Freedom* came back to life. Propulsion systems, lights, environmental, and weapons systems, all began recharging quickly. Pleased with myself, I hurried above and scanned the area to be sure that no Wolfen or other ships were near me. Then I set the navicomputer to the task of calculating a course back to Viste. Once that task had begun, I went back below and quickly secured the alien metal object with a cargo net to keep it from rolling free and accidentally touching another cable or anything else during our return trip. Interestingly, the metal showed no sign of having been charged or having in any way stored the energy it had been bleeding from the ship during that time period. It would be challenging to study it further.

Having secured my ship again, I returned above and set my

full attention on the trip back to Viste. I'd already had enough close calls that day to hold me for a while.

It was a relief to hail Port Viste some hours later, and my ID codes assured that I would not be hampered from touching down without delay. Instead of going to the *Freedom*'s berth in the port, I took her directly to my work area at the base of Drakyn's mountain. Before I even touched down, I had called Gall via the link and urged him to make his way to my workshop quickly to see something he would find fascinating. I then locked down the ship's systems and popped the hatch to find Drakyn himself standing there, arms crossed over his chest and a forbidding expression on his face.

"Hi sweetie," I greeted him innocently. "Miss me? You've got to see what I—"

"Are you injured?" he interrupted, taking a quick step toward me that made me automatically step back slightly.

"No. Why would I be injured?" I asked as I frowned slightly at him, honestly puzzled. "Is something wrong?"

Drakyn had already extended a hand toward me, but then he stopped himself and closed his eyes momentarily as if to regain control. "Honor," he said, "All day I have been picking up very strong impressions of extreme and imminent danger from your mind. What have you been doing?"

"That's weird. I haven't been sending you any messages...," I began, but then paused before demanding, "You just *tune in* on my thoughts any time you want to? How dare you!"

He was frowning now, and he continued speaking with quiet, dangerous-sounding intensity, "Yes, I can, Honor. I thought I made you understand, we are very closely linked by blood and spirit since your rebirth as one of my kind. You can learn to do the same thing, to reach out and touch my mind from unbelievable distances..."

"So even my thoughts aren't my own anymore? I have no privacy at all?" I interjected. I knew I was being unreasonable, but the idea of him monitoring my brain really irritated me.

Stiffly, Drakyn hissed, "You can also learn to shield your thoughts from me, or from anyone wishing to invade your privacy. Honor, I want you to tell me what happened today!" He caught my arm and gave me a slight shake.

Yanking free of his touch, I snarled, "Save yourself some time! Just crawl in my head and get your answers! Drakyn, I hate when you get proprietary with me! You know that!"

Drakyn looked down at me frostily. "I was concerned about your welfare, Honor. Only that." He then turned with a swirl of his black cloak and stalked away from the work area without so much as a glance back at me.

I stood and watched him go, tears pricking at my eyes, feeling foolish and childishly selfish, but my own pride would not allow me to go after him and apologize.

A few moments later Gall appeared, grumbling that he had to come all the way to the castle when there was a perfectly good berth at the port. My touchy temper made me snarl at him angrily enough that he subsided in surprise and listened in silence to my account of the incident with the disappearing asteroid ship, and how bringing aboard a piece of that ship had affected the *Freedom*. Then I took him into the cargo hold with me, to bring the metallic sample out so we could begin tests on it.

My temper cooled with my enthusiasm for the work we were doing. I was not hungry enough to join Gall hours later when the engineer declared that he needed to get some food and then rest for the night. He promised to re-join me first thing in the morning and I did not try to keep him there with me. I was too engrossed in the spectral analysis I was running on the metal to be distracted by him for very long. The results were giving me ideas about possible uses for the metal that might result in wonderful tools or terrible weapons. It would be imperative to keep this stuff a secret. With that realization, I knew it was equally important that Drakyn hear about what I had discovered. I had already gotten up from my worktable and brushed myself off before I began to consider just how annoyed he had been when he left me earlier. I had started the fight, and it was time for me to do something about making peace again. Sometimes my temper irritated even me.

I secured my work area with double locks and then proceeded up the long staircase to the castle above, shaking my head at my own actions. I knew that Drakyn had merely been concerned about my welfare. Why did I have to get so prickly with him? Was I this touchy before I became a blood drinker? I did not think so! Much as I loved Drakyn and as much as I did not think he would purposely hurt me, he was nevertheless still intimidating enough that I did not look forward to approaching him with this apology. He had repeatedly told me that he was a solitary creature for many years before my arrival in his life. Accommodating my presence was a constant effort for a being like Drakyn. I knew it was because he cared for me. He was physically and mentally strong enough to squash me like a particularly annoying insect if he was so inclined.

Reaching the castle corridors, I realized that I was dusty and smudged with oil and soot from my efforts in the workshop, so I headed for my own rooms to bathe before going to Drakyn.

I was startled to find Drakyn awaiting me in my rooms when I got there. He was sitting in the big chair nearest the lit fireplace, and he looked long and hard at me when I entered, then silently returned his intense gaze to the fire. A crystal goblet in his left hand was half-full of a red liquid that I suspected was pure blood, and I hoped it was from an animal rather than some higher-order being.

"Drakyn! Hello." My greeting sounded inane, but it was not well thought-out. "Drakyn, I'm sorry I—"

He tossed the crystal goblet into the fire and it shattered with a musical tinkle. Drakyn then got to his feet and came toward me purposefully, with one hand outstretched.

I wanted to run out of the room, but I did not allow myself to do that. This time I would accept his bad temper, so I stood there passively as he took hold of my arm, none too gently. He dragged me close to him, and snarled, "What am I going to do with you, woman? What?" He shook me sharply.

When he paused and actually wanted a reply from me, I said softly, "Drakyn, I don't know what to tell you. We keep locking horns over my independence, and you keep telling me I have all the freedom I wish. Then you turn around and monitor me, and treat me like a helpless child after I've been out of your sight pursuing my own interests!"

"In your life as a protein consumer, you *ARE* a child!" Drakyn informed me with another shake. "You need to learn to be disciplined and controlled…" Drakyn's free hand was upon the buckle of the thick belt he wore around his waist as if he intended to remove it and use it on me.

"What kind of discipline do your birth people use for their young ones?" I asked, fighting to remain calm myself this time. My heart was pounding. "Do you beat your children? Your students? Lock them up? Spy on them mentally so you know what happens to them at all times? Would it really make you feel better, like a good teacher, to use that strap on me? Is that what you want?" Intending to startle him into reason, I reached up behind my back and used my own considerable strength to rip my tunic open in the back, then half-turned to offer my back to him. "Go ahead and do it, if it would satisfy you! But only if you're prepared for what it will do to our relationship. I'm sure you know just how hard to beat me to achieve...*discipline*!"

I realized I had made a mistake in trying to call his bluff when Drakyn's dark eyes blazed a startling red and he grabbed me hard enough to make me cry out softly. It seriously worried me to see his eyes burning that way, and my survival instincts warned me that I could be badly injured by his unleashed temper. His hands were like stone and I could not even begin to resist him as he dragged me out into the corridor. When I began to protest, he ignored me completely and forced me with him up a set of stone stairs I knew led to his set of rooms in the tower. Reaching the top, he kicked open the door that led into his sitting room. Then he slammed the door shut as he pulled me through to the bedroom. No lamp and no fire was lit, and the shutters had been secured. Thus, when he slammed that second door, it put us in complete darkness. His grip on me did not lessen and I heard him turn a metal lock on the door.

I could not see anything; even my enhanced night vision was useless in such a complete lack of illumination. My heart was thundering in my ears, but I made absolutely no effort to struggle. The effort would have been useless against his great strength.

Then Drakyn shoved me face-down onto the bed and, putting a heavy knee at the small of my back, he ripped my tunic entirely away. Next, he dragged off my trousers and boots as well.

I tried to speak and reason with Drakyn to get control of himself. Ignoring me, he used pieces of my tunic to secure my wrists to what I guessed were the bedposts. More concerned now, I wanted to fight him tooth and nail, to promise never to upset him that way again, but my own pride and something else told me that motionless silence would be far wiser. I wished there was a light.

He was leaning close over me and I felt his warm breath and occasionally his long hair touching my back. Finally, I could hear him unbuckle and pull off that big belt strap. The pressure of his knee was removed from my back as he stood up nearby.

Braced for pain, I shivered uncontrollably when I felt him lightly trail that leather strap over my backbone. I whispered his name appealingly, my voice breaking with the need to sob.

His big hand pressed the back of my neck as he hissed: "Silence! Keep quiet and still, woman, I'm warning you!"

I subsided to silence again, yet I heard him moving close by me. I jumped like a startled cat when he climbed onto the bed nude, his knees straddling my hips.

You fear me. Why don't you resist me? His thoughts entered my mind as his hands rested heavily upon my shoulders, pinning me down. *Answer me—without speaking!*

The worry I was experiencing made it difficult not to speak aloud, but I took his warning seriously. Gathering my wits, I reached toward him with my mind to connect with him, to try to soothe and reason with him, and found...amusement! At my involuntary reaction of shocked outrage, I felt my entire being surrounded with warmth and affection and a larger emotion that flooded his brain and then spilled into my own like sweet nectar. Still stunned by this realization, his big hands slipped beneath me, cupping my bare breasts and he began kissing first my neck and shoulders, and then he moved down along the line of my spine. Those hands leisurely explored my breasts, my belly, and lower still, until I was breathing hard. Then he lifted my hips slightly as he suddenly pressed himself into me from behind. I whimpered softly with the first connection and then gasped aloud when he began to move himself irresistibly within my flesh, combining his passion with my own rising need until both of us were crying out in unison of pleasure.

When at last our breathing slowed to normal, I lay still upon my stomach, with his big body draped over mine. One of his hands played in strands of my hair, running them between his fingertips. The other hand smoothed the skin of my back where he occasionally pressed kisses.

"Drakyn...," I began, wanting again to apologize to him for my childish attitude earlier.

His fingers covered my lips to stop the words. "Silence, woman," he rumbled deeply, seriously. "Understand this: not one more spoken word between us this night!"

I understood what he was saying to me: words were not really necessary between the two of us. I could communicate volumes of information to him and receive the same from him by simply linking my mind with his. He had asked me earlier why I had not tried to fight him and I now communicated that, despite the worry at his rough approach, I had not felt any serious intention to hurt me emanating from his mind. I had been reading the texture of his thoughts instinctively, rather than making an actual decision to do so. I now realized that the spoken word was an impediment to communication for those linked as we were. Drakyn and I could understand each other's fears, anticipate each other's desires and needs, and fulfill them without uttering a single word. Drakyn could not separate his concern for me and for my safety from the concern he felt for his own body. We were one intense entity, far beyond the cellular level.

We spent the remainder of the dark hours making love with each other in ways that were both familiar and foreign to my experience. By communicating intent and love without words, I again found I trusted and loved Drakyn in ways I would never have thought possible. It was one of the most erotic nights I had ever experienced up to that point in my life. My body always tired much more quickly than Drakyn's, and at last I needed and did surrender to sleep, still in his arms.

Drakyn was not in the room when I awakened in the morning. Dim sunlight came around the wooden shutters that had blocked the moonlight. My hands had been freed hours earlier, but now I smiled when I noticed that my destroyed tunic was still tied to the bedpost and I realized that I could have easily torn myself free of those bonds last night had I truly tried to defend myself. His actions might have appeared brutal, but considering the kind of violence of which he was capable, Drakyn was particularly careful not to hurt me. He understood that, sometimes, the only way he could deal with my obstinate nature was to completely overwhelm me. He had already said that only a physical demonstration of his power over me would serve to impress me. Last night he proved his point.

I was much wiser after that night.

I decided to take a long, soaking bath in the deep bathing pool in the adjoining room. In the back of my mind I was hoping that Drakyn might return while I was there and join me in the warm water for a while. However, he didn't appear and after spending more than enough time in the water, I got out and reached for one of the drying cloths on the nearby shelves. Still deep in my rather unruly thoughts, I did not hear the door open as I moved in that direction. Instead of reaching the towels, I literally bumped into a fur-covered figure that had stepped into the bathing room.

"Honor!" Tarquin hissed, his muscular arms closing around me for a moment to steady me when I would have fallen backward in alarm. He blinked down at me in surprise equal to my own as I stepped back from his furry form. The Malkin felinoid made no move to turn his back, but the fur at the back of his neck had ruffled up and his whiskers arched as he involuntarily took in my scent. "I apologize. I was told Lord Drakyn was here. This is not appropriate! I will go now…"

"He left around dawn, Tarquin." I answered him quickly, picking up a towel. I resisted turning my back to him; I had already learned that doing so was an insult to Malkin males.

"I apologize for the intrusion." Tarquin said, and he left quickly.

When he was gone, I could not help but smile at his stiff formality despite the fact that he was obviously interested in looking at me. Human females were, after all, in short supply around here, so I could not fault such curiosity in someone who was essentially a giant cat.

Later that day, after several hours with my new project, I sought Drakyn in his rooms and his gymnasium, and then finally located him at the Port offices, deep in a consultation with Pried ker D'at and a few others. Drakyn acknowledged my arrival with a lingering glance, but continued giving directions regarding some sticky-sounding fee negotiation. It was a few ticks before he dismissed the people from his office.

Without even a greeting, Drakyn asked me, "Have you found

any further information on that alloy you brought back with you, Honor? You look like you have news."

Sitting on the edge of the desk, I grinned at him. "It's going to work, Drakyn," I told him, trying to control the excitement I felt. "Of course, it'll need to be strictly controlled and tested, but I know I can make it work!"

Taking my hand, Drakyn squeezed it rather tightly as he said, "We must be careful about this, Honor. You are on the verge of creating a device that can effectively hide a ship from scanners, creating a shield that is the next best thing to invisibility. Many, many powers would murder entire planets for such a tool, and destroy even more if they took possession of it. This could become a terrible weapon for invading forces."

In seriousness I replied, "I know that, Drakyn. I still haven't even explained to Gall what I'm trying to do. He thinks I'm testing the metal for use as a heat shield. I really doubt that he suspects anything else, because I keep talking about using it to protect the *Freedom*'s shields for a long-term trip, back to Fleet territories. He keeps grumbling to me that the *Freedom* is too small to even attempt such a trip!"

"It is," Drakyn remarked, putting my hand to his mouth briefly. His blood teeth were slightly enlarged and they scraped against my skin, startling me, but I smiled in spite of myself as I also felt his desire.

Not even trying to pull back from him, I asked, "What is it, Drakyn? What's wrong?"

"You need a bigger ship to work with, to see if the energy deflection is as powerful as you think it is, don't you?" he asked, but not waiting for an answer from me. "And, you'll need a crew for a larger ship as well."

"I won't need a crew unless I'm…going somewhere?" I wondered aloud. I turned the hand he held and wrapped my own fingers through his. "Tell me what's bothering you?"

He stood towering over me. "It seems I must let you go," he said simply.

"Do you want to be rid of me?" I asked.

He glared fire at me. "Of course not!"

I made a face back at him. "Then don't be maudlin and dramatic, sweetie. I might go away for a while, but you'll never rid yourself of me! I'm in your blood, you know, and vice versa, eh?" I showed him my own teeth.

He wrapped his big, sheltering arms around me and held me close against his chest. "Dangerous, difficult female," he remarked in a fond tone.

"You bet!" I agreed, relaxing against him. Some inner demon made me ask, "Drakyn, do you know if Malkin males and Terran females are sexually compatible?"

"What?" He stepped back, but kept his hands on me, staring hard.

I started laughing in spite of myself. It was fun to tease him when he was so serious.

The rest of that week was spent in concentrated effort down at my workshop, scarcely taking time to see Drakyn, even for meals. The Lord of Viste seemed to understand now, and he often came down to see me at odd moments, generally late at night when Gall had gone off to sleep. I was so engrossed by what I knew would be a successful effort, that I really did not take much note of the time or day, of meals or anything else. Only when my need for protein became impossible to ignore did I do anything to assuage it with quickly-produced computer synthetics that I gulped down without really tasting them.

I had just upended a half-liter container of liquid protein one night when Drakyn spoke my name close by, making me jump visibly. When I turned to face him a bit impatiently, I was struck as usual by how good looking the Lord of Viste was in his dark and sober clothing, with the long cape pushed back over his shoulders.

"Evening, sweetie," I greeted him, tossing the protein bottle into a recycling unit. "You really shouldn't sneak up on me like that..."

"I want you to come with me," he announced without preamble, his face its usual emotionless mask. He held out a hand to me, crooking his fingers almost impatiently.

Resisting the instinctive urge to be difficult, I accepted his hand while asking, "What is it, Drakyn? Is something wrong?"

"Not at all," he replied as a molecular transport wave suddenly surrounded us, and then took us away from the mountainside ship's berth. This startled me because Drakyn disliked such transportation. The energy wave generally clouds the vision for a few seconds, and this time when my sight cleared I found myself upon the bridge of an unfamiliar ship of human design!

"Drakyn, where are we?" I wondered aloud.

Releasing my hand, Drakyn gestured widely around the area, saying, "This is your new ship, Honor. Effective at once." He smiled faintly at me.

"Mine?"

"Yes. I assume you'll want it. Come here and look at the statistical analysis of the ship. I think it will be more than adequate for your needs." He drew me with him to a post that was obviously used for navigation and engineering. A few touches to the computer pad, and the screen before us began to spout information that made my mouth drop open slightly. This was clearly a starship—and it was unquestionably capable of inter-stellar system travel!

All I could think to say was: "I will need a crew..."

"Undoubtedly," he responded without pause. "I believe ten individuals will do."

I actually startled Drakyn when I turned to him and threw my arms around his neck and hugged him energetically, saying, "You are so good to me! I love you, Drakyn! I love you!"

It would have been the perfect moment for him to echo my sentiments, but instead Drakyn merely held me close against him, his face above mine so I could not see his expression. For some reason I picked up extreme sadness, a kind of loneliness from him in that moment. I truly wanted to find a way to change that, but I was at a loss as to what I might do, so I just held him closer. I instinctively knew that I must not try to get Drakyn to talk about what made him so solemn.

Knowing the future has that effect upon a person.

Chapter 9

The Crew

GALL was the first enthusiastic volunteer to join my crew, followed closely by two other engineers with whom I had become acquainted during my work in Viste's port area. It was not easy to choose the kind of people I wanted to man my ship; I already knew which of them had less than honest intentions and would try to steal the ship from me at their first opportunity. Unfortunately, Port Viste attracted mostly that sort of clientele. Eventually I learned that Gall was a very good judge of character, and I allowed him to do the scouting for me.

I did find one crew member myself in the main hangars one day. He was a young humanoid originally from Andromeda colony. He had been captured during a raid by an Andree/Coryan ship on a cargo tug, aboard which he was one of four crew members. The others were killed in the fight, and the Coryan commander almost eliminated the teenage boy they captured. Then the commander had second thoughts because of the lad's extremely handsome, almost effeminate good looks. It was decided to make him a slave, with the intent of selling him to a certain wealthy ship's captain whose tastes ran in that direction.

My attention was drawn to the boy when he broke away from his guard and ran desperately across the staging area, taking shelter among some crates near the *Freedom* shuttle. Two burly

Coryans had already grabbed and dragged the boy out into the open, raining blows on his shoulders and back, when I stepped forward to intervene. Not in a mood to waste time with words, I used a length of pipe applied to the nearest Coryan's equivalent of a solar plexus to gain their full attention.

By this time a crowd had begun to gather, calling out encouragement to us, doubtless hoping for a fight of some kind. I had just stepped forward to demand the Coryan's attention when the second one turned aggressively toward me, still keeping a hold upon his captive. Perhaps it was lucky for the Coryan that more than one of the port regulars took hold of him to restrain him before he touched me. I heard Drakyn's name spoken several times in alien languages, in hushed tones. The Coryan holding the boy looked visibly ill and he hesitated as if undecided what to do next.

Feeling slightly foolish myself for the aggression I showed, I spoke up in a pleasant tone, "This young man is intended as a slave, is he not? I wish to speak with your captain, please." Even as I said this, the Coryan I faced was looking over my shoulder at someone else. Turning, I found myself regarding a familiar face: Chivv R.

To give him credit, the Coryan commander did not show the thoughts in his mind. "You have survived and even thrived, I see," Chivv R remarked softly. He gestured for his own guards to relax behind him.

"No thanks to your efforts," I countered coldly, automatically noting his slight limp. That had not been there during our last encounter. I wondered if his leg was regrown, or a transplant. "The boy there, he's your—for lack of a better word—prize?"

"He is, just as you were," the Coryan pirate replied calmly, his gaze steady upon me.

Aware of the hopelessly frightened look on the young human's face, I asked quietly, "His price?"

Amusement flickered across Chivv's coldly handsome face before he replied, "To the mistress of the Lord of Viste, I present him as a gift!" He gestured for his men to bring the terrified teenager forward.

Allowing my face to appear equally amused, I inclined my head and murmured, "The commander is most generous. Thank you, Chivv R."

"In return I ask only one *small* favor," the Coryan added gently as he touched the boy's manacles with the clear rod I remembered very well.

"Ah. Yes?" I prompted, "What is your favor, Chivv?" I noted that the manacles fell from the boy's wrists and I could see the impulse to flee again building within the boy's body. To calm him, I smiled powerfully and extended a hand to him in a gesture of invitation and reassurance. The lad hesitated only a moment before accepting my hand and letting me draw him to stand slightly behind me.

Smiling continuously, Chivv answered me: "I request only the joy of your company, your conversation, possibly over a goblet of wine?" His golden eyes met mine in a clear challenge.

Laughing, I replied, "I no longer drink the kind of wine you do, Chivv. But if you wish conversation with me, I will meet you over in that bar shortly." I gestured to a nearby building, and did not bother to watch the blink of surprise on Chivv's face as I turned to the boy. "What is your name?"

He had a thick shock of light brown hair and his amazing lavender-colored eyes were huge in his thin face. In a surprisingly deep voice, he replied, "Seca Fordivite. I do thank you for your help, ma'am, but I won't willingly agree to be *anybody's* slave!" He clenched his fists as if preparing to do battle with me now.

In a gentle tone, I said, "I don't own or want any slaves, Seca. You have your freedom, but in a port like this one, you will need a source of income to survive and support yourself. I am offering you a job."

His beautiful eyes widened for a brief moment of hope, but then experience made him murmur cautiously, "What sort of job?"

"I recently acquired an interstellar class ship, and I'm in the process of refitting it, and gathering a crew," I told him quite honestly. "I need an assistant to help in several ways during this process. If we get along, you might join my crew. What kind of work have you done in the past?"

For a moment Seca's face showed the pain of memory, but then he swallowed hard and said, "My brother and I were navigators. I was junior and helped him monitor the sensors, and took over during relief shifts. Our tug was pretty much automated, but I understand computers and I learn quickly. I would like that job, if you're offering it."

Within a few ticks I had installed Seca inside the *Freedom* shuttle with instructions to guard it, and to call me if anyone touched it. Of course, no one would dare to tamper with my shuttle because of Drakyn, but Seca did not know this yet. With that matter settled, I glared strongly at the two Coryans who had been abusing Seca. They wisely realized that it would be best for them to depart the area. Then I went to the bar where I had sent Chivv R.

It was noisy, smoky, and crowded inside, as usual. My entrance made no visible impression upon its regular patrons. I had often come there with Gall or Pried, or both, and the bartenders knew what kind of synthetic to serve me. Nodding to several acquaintances en route, I made my way to the table where Chivv awaited me. The only reason I went there was to satisfy my curiosity, but I also reminded myself that the Coryan pheromone-thrill could still hit me when I wasn't prepared to block it. Chivv watched me carefully with those interesting eyes as I slipped into the seat opposite him.

Without preamble, I began, "So, I hope you don't hold what happened in the past against me, Chivv. I really don't have time for threats or silly talk of revenge."

Raising his brows in surprise, the Coryan replied, "Certainly not! It was our mistake to underestimate you because you were female. I was doubly mistaken not to have offered you an opportunity to join my crew. I shan't repeat such a mistake again, should a similar opportunity present itself."

"How generous of you," I commented, glancing down at his leg, visible through the glass tabletop. "My blaster shot took your leg, didn't it?"

Chivv inclined his head in agreement and smiled unexpectedly at me. "That's the nature of the game, Honor. It's re-grown quite well. I have not returned here for many cycles. Imagine my wonder upon learning that the little human slave-prize I thought had been killed in a crash did not die! Fates can be most unpredictable."

"Yes," I agreed soberly, "They can be."

Leaning closer to me, he went on, "And then I learned more. I learned that you had acquired a ship of your own! That you come and go freely from this port, and are under the Lord of Viste's personal protection, and now you seek a crew for an even larger ship. A being like myself has cause to wonder at the purpose of such an enterprise."

"I am sure you do," I countered, smiling at him with real amusement. "My home is in Fleet-protected space. I plan to return there."

Chivv's big green hand came down over mine unexpectedly. I started to yank it back to protect myself, but then stopped, caught by the intensity of his gaze. Very softly, Chivv R said, "There is talk of a Wolfen commander. This commander came by his command when his own lord was killed here on Viste not long ago. Probably by Lord Drakyn. It is said that his throat was torn open, and his blood was supped upon."

"What is your point, Chivv?" I demanded coldly, but felt my heart begin to race.

"This new Wolfen commander wishes to learn information from whoever can provide it. He wishes to know what has become of the human woman belonging to Drakyn here on Viste. He inquires into the possibility of persuading an independent agent to find this woman, possibly even to abduct her for him. The price he offers is high. He seems to have a reason for particular interest in this female." Chivv's voice was dry with sarcasm.

"Why are you telling me this, Chivv?" I asked forthrightly.

Releasing my hand, he made a deprecating gesture. "The Wolfen is a coward, and surely a fool to risk Drakyn's fury. I dislike both cowards and fools."

Smiling widely at him, I remarked, "And to think I believed that pirates were only interested in profit!"

"It would be dangerous for you to leave Drakyn's protection around Viste," Chivv pointed out.

Shaking my head, I replied, "Space is huge, Chivv. Viste is quite small in comparison, and even Drakyn cannot constantly protect me. I do that for myself very well. How do you suppose the first Wolfen commander really died? I assure you, Chivv, Drakyn did not kill him!" I allowed him to glimpse my involuntarily extended blood teeth for a moment. Inwardly I was amazed that I could speak so lightly about that ugly incident.

Chivv's golden eyes widened slightly before he muttered, "It has been said of you, but I doubted it until now. Drakyn must have been very impressed with you!"

"Try not to be insulting, even if you mean it as a compliment," I suggested lightly, accepting the goblet of red liquid protein that the auto-serve unit produced just then. Chivv's rather alarmed expression made me laugh in spite of myself. "I'd like to believe there is peace between us, Chivv. Is there? I will trust your word to be true on the issue; you've demonstrated it can be relied upon in the past."

"Peace it is, Honor," Chivv pledged, grasping my wrist as he would have done with a male.

***

THE young Andromedan, Seca Fordivite, proved to be a treasure. While I understood the design and mechanics of ship building, Seca understood computers better than any being I had ever encountered, and was able to teach others with ease. He even impressed Gall of Tredar the first time we gave him access to a computer console. It was not long before the best mechanic in the universe routinely consulted with Seca, as we proceeded with our overhaul of the ship I had begun to call the *Serpentine*. In just over the one solar year it required to complete the ship's refit, Seca taught me more about computers than I had learned in my four years at the Fleet Academy. I now owed most of my computer knowledge to that intelligent teenager.

My young friend, Merlin, was already entering felinoid adolescence as work drew closer to completion. His interest in and talent for piloting grew more evident every day. Merlin and Seca became fast friends almost from the moment they met, so the felinoid youth spent much of his time around the *Serpentine* as well. In response to Merlin's repeated requests, I began to take the youngster with me when I went up in the *Freedom*. When I allowed Merlin to take the controls, I could see that piloting the ship was as natural as breathing to him. I could relate completely to the hunger in his eyes every time Merlin set eyes upon a maneuverable ship like the *Freedom*. He had a steady temper and an even steadier paw on the controls that would have impressed even my Academy instructors. Merlin was good enough to give any of my classmates at the Planetary Fleet Academy a run for their money. So I came to realize that, when I made my trip home, Merlin must be among those who would accompany me.

I had often told Merlin my personal history, and the felinoid was always fascinated with the training I had received at the Fleet Academy. As he matured, he began fantasizing aloud about how he would react to this or that if he were ever allowed to attend the Academy and become a pilot. In taking Merlin with me, I fully intended to deliver him to an environment that would assure the educational experience he obviously desired. When I worried aloud to Drakyn about how Tarquin and Cinna might react if the one they now considered their child became a student at the Fleet Academy, Drakyn dismissed my concern with a wave of his hand.

"Honor," Drakyn reproved me gently, "Tarquin knows what the boy is dreaming about. Tarquin has raised no objection. He will not. Merlin is free to choose his own path."

Chapter 10

A Visitor

HONOR was happy. She was enjoying rebuilding the starship *Serpentine*, teaching Merlin to fly, and gathering a crew that she knew would work well together. Only when she stopped and thought seriously about it, did she consider that everything she was doing would eventually take her far from Viste, and far from Drakyn. That realization left her feeling cold, slightly sick in the pit of her stomach and missing him already. She was also a bit afraid of how much control she would maintain when she was away from his influence and support. This did not stop her, however.

Her experiments with the odd metal composite she had obtained were proceeding smoothly, despite the fact that she had only briefly tinkered with it. She only turned to that project whenever she wanted to relax and think of something other than her planned trip back to Fleet space. She knew instinctively that if she put her full attention to this mystery, the light would go on in her brain and she would solve the puzzle. She kept her progress a strict secret, not even telling Gall what she was doing and saying little about it to Drakyn. In any case, Drakyn did not ask about her progress with it, apparently trusting her to tell him if anything requiring his attention occurred.

Honor still loved going off on solo flights (or semi-solo flights, if she took Merlin with her), just to explore the system surrounding Viste. She visited the three other planets, all uninhabited, with rocky, atmosphere-free or gaseous environments. Then she ventured a bit further, to the edges of Border Space near the Wolfen territories. There were several pirate settlements in this area, and she enjoyed taking a few chances with the occasional Coryan, Malkin, or other species' vessels she encountered — effectively playing cat and mouse, at times. She considered these to be exercises in honing her skills, but told Drakyn nothing about them — at least not verbally. Honor knew that he still mentally listened in on her activities. He was unable to keep himself from doing so, and she defiantly held nothing back from him. Instead, she rather flippantly challenged him to try and interfere with her forays. At times she could sense his frustration with her, but he never again attempted to restrain her actions.

One morning, about three months before her scheduled departure date, Honor planned to go out on one of her exploratory runs for the day in the *Freedom*. Merlin was to accompany her, and she agreed to let the young felinoid handle every aspect of their trip. He would conduct the craft's physical inspection, plot the course to a planetoid security outpost halfway across the system, and also pilot the *Freedom* during the trip. Knowing Merlin would need a bit of time, Honor left him busy doing his pre-flight checks while she quietly sought out Tarquin back at Drakyn's fortress. She knew the big felinoid would be busy in his security office at that time of the morning. Honor parked her land vehicle outside and went in through the public entrance without bothering to tell Drakyn that she had returned. When she entered his office, Tarquin looked at her with as much surprise as any felinoid could show.

Smiling at him, Honor spoke up, "I apologize for dropping in on you unannounced, Tarquin, but I wanted to let you know something before Merlin and I go out in the *Freedom* today…"

The great felinoid's prehensile tail wrapped around his right front paw, involuntarily expressing some nervousness for a moment as he said, "Welcome, Lady Honor, at any time. Sit, if you wish. I was given to understand than you had already left the port."

Perching on the edge of a chair near him, Honor could not

help but smile at Tarquin. She regarded him as the equivalent of a giant pussycat, despite the four-inch fangs that extended over his lower lip. He was a kind-hearted and tolerant parent for Merlin, and also quite proud of him.

Quickly, Honor said, "I want to let you know that Merlin is doing all of the piloting on the trip today. If he performs as satisfactorily as I expect, I would like to recommend that he be allowed to undergo the standard Malkin pilot's examination and become licensed."

Tarquin arched his whiskers thoughtfully, but Honor could tell by the way his pupils dilated from slits that he was pleased. "Have you told Merlin this?" he inquired.

"No. Why put pressure on him? He'll get nervous enough when he does take the pilot's exam," Honor countered evenly. "Do you object, Tarquin?"

The big felinoid licked the back of his left paw quickly before replying, "Of course not, my lady. You have instructed the cub better than anyone else might have done. I thank you for this, and for your plans to take Merlin with you to the Fleet Academy. It is a great joy to see such achievement in one so young."

"Thank you, Tarquin—" Honor began, but paused when the communicator on her belt sounded with Merlin's voice reporting that all pre-flight checks were near completion. She got to her feet, acknowledged Merlin's call, and then said, "Tarquin, the boy has talent. It must be nurtured."

"He has a patient and gifted teacher in you, Lady Honor," Tarquin replied rather formally, and then suddenly inquired, "Are you proceeding back to the Port now, to leave?"

Nodding, Honor replied, "Yes. Why? Do you want me to give Merlin a message?"

Raising a paw, Tarquin licked it again rather nervously before saying, "Not at all. I merely wondered what to tell Lord Drakyn…"

Chuckling, Honor answered, "Don't worry about saying anything to him. I already took my leave of him for the day. See you later, Tarq!" Grinning to herself, she left the offices, and went back out to her vehicle.

That was when Honor spotted Drakyn up on one of the balconies that overlooked the valley on the south side of the complex.

At first she thought he was alone, but then Honor realized that another figure occupied the balcony and she grew very curious. The balcony was four flights up and angled away from where she stood, but it appeared as if the other large figure with Drakyn was deliberately hanging back in a shadowed area, almost as if unwilling to be spotted by others. Honor suspected that few people would have been able to see him at all, unless gifted with the enhanced eyesight she now commanded. It was a large male, dressed entirely in black, much as Drakyn generally preferred to do.

Curious, Honor did not even hesitate to act. She moved swiftly back inside the fortress and ran easily up the four flights of stairs toward the general area where she knew she would find Drakyn and his guest. As she drew near, a line about "curiosity killing cats" went through her mind, but she ignored the caution because she was now actively wondering what Drakyn did whenever he left her company, or when she left his to pursue her own activities. When she reached the right floor, she found herself facing a corridor with which she was unfamiliar. She knew this area held a suite of offices, but she had no idea who might occupy them. There were four doors evenly spaced on either side of the hall, but all of them were shut and it was silent.

Resisting the urge to call out to him with her mind, Honor instead spoke aloud and asked, "Drakyn? Are you here? Drakyn?"

Only silence met her ears for a tick or two, but then she made out the low rumble of male voices behind one of the doors. Something made Honor go to a door immediately beside that one and silently let herself in. It was empty of anything but a desk, but it did have a balcony very similar to the one outside the room next door. The exterior door slid open silently, and suddenly Honor could overhear the conversation from the next balcony.

Honor had no idea why she felt compelled to be circumspect about approaching Drakyn and his unknown companion; she simply knew she must. Repeatedly, she tried to "tune in" to Drakyn's mind, but she found herself being quite effectively blocked. Perhaps it was frustration in response to this failure that made her want to find out more despite this resistance. So she proceeded as silently as possible, slipping back into the hallway, through the next office door and over to the balcony door. Now she was blocking her own thoughts and emotions from being read by Drakyn, should he try to do so. It would serve him right.

Holding her breath, she pushed the pressure-sensitive door release and watched as it soundlessly rolled back, letting in a burst of fresh mountain air. Immediately she could hear the low rumble of Drakyn's rich baritone voice as he declared, "You're taking a ridiculous risk even being here!"

There was a pause and the almost soundless yet unmistakable creak of leather clothing just before another voice, as deep as Drakyn's and yet roughened as if with emotion or some old throat injury, spoke in a tone just above a hiss: "I saw her as clearly as I see you now!"

"I do not dispute the facts," Drakyn replied with silky dangerousness. "You nevertheless must leave here..."

"You cannot keep her, Drakyn! You must not!" The tone was like a whiplash upon bare skin.

Drakyn's voice indicated that he was unimpressed by the violence of emotion he was confronting. "It is YOU who must not interfere! This time is MINE, completely and without interference. Understand this: if one variable is altered in the slightest, then all future variables will be similarly affected! You must know and understand this! Are you willing to gamble with the future?"

Honor somehow felt that she was the subject of this conversation and she wanted to confront Drakyn and whoever the other person was with him. She wanted to insist upon an explanation. It occurred in the back of her mind that she was being incredibly arrogant in assuming the conversation had anything to do with her, but she could not argue with her own intuition.

The two men began talking again, but suddenly it was as if they were using a language that Honor had never heard before and had no reference to understand.

Honor instantly knew that Drakyn had somehow become aware of her presence and was now managing to interfere with her comprehension. She stepped forward, intending to confront them and demand to know what was going on. For a moment Honor was able to focus upon Drakyn, and then she turned her eyes toward the other person, one considerably taller and even broader of shoulder than Drakyn.

At that moment Honor lost consciousness and collapsed at

Drakyn's feet as if stunned by a weapon.

The large stranger uttered an alarmed oath and moved as if to gather up the woman.

Drakyn put himself between them while spitting out the words, "Do NOT touch her! She is unhurt. She is merely unconscious. Leave this place. Leave her to me!"

"How did she know to come here? . . . You did this to her!"

Inclining his head, Drakyn said ironically, "You underestimate her. I am protecting what is mine, what is hers, and what will yet be immeasurably important for us all. Honor will remember nothing of this encounter." He looked down at the woman, saying, as he did, "Go now. Do not delay further…"

**

"HONOR, what are you doing here?" came a muffled voice, as if from some distance away.

Honor blinked and shook herself free from a reverie of thought about Merlin's talents, and then lifted her chin to regard Drakyn standing beside her vehicle. He was in his shirt sleeves as if he had been using his sword for exercise, and he looked down at her with a tiny frown between his brows.

"Is something wrong, little one?" he demanded.

"Wrong? N-No. I was just…thinking about something for a tick." Honor shook her head and then rubbed her left knee; it was stinging as if she had bumped or fallen onto it.

Drakyn leaned close to her and his lips grazed hers almost roughly for a moment. "I thought you were going out in the *Freedom* with Merlin this morning," he said, with his dark eyes intense and compelling.

"I am. I am! I just came back here to talk with Tarquin for a tick about Merlin. I'm going now. I'll probably see you tonight."

Straightening up, Drakyn said, "Of course you will. Return safely, Honor."

Grinning up at him, Honor replied, "Always, sweetie. Bye again." Then she powered up the vehicle and guided it back onto the roadway.

Drakyn stood and watched until the vehicle had gone around a curve in the roadway and was out of sight. Then he retrieved his dark coat from behind the row of bushes where he had dropped it, and headed back into the fortress. His heart was heavy with deliberately forgotten knowledge that had been returning to him in great quantity in recent days.

Chapter 11

Separation

MERLIN made me very proud the day I decided to let him test his piloting skills. It was a good thing that he knew what he was doing, because I began to develop a strange headache even before we left Viste that morning. At first I thought nothing of it, but as it grew more intense I began to worry a bit. I did not remember having any headaches since beginning my new life with Drakyn on Viste. Regardless, by the time we reached the security outpost that was our objective, I was somewhat distracted.

Once we had successfully landed in the small port, Merlin sent a routine report back to Port Viste, informing security that we had reached our destination.

I was scanning the port directory screen, somehow convinced that only one thing would relieve my headache: fresh, non-synthetic animal protein. I had no idea why the idea was in my throbbing head, but I was not about to argue with it at that moment. We had scarcely landed in the port when I stood up, saying, "You take care of our lock-down, Merlin. I need to go outside for a few breaths of fresh air…" Then I popped the hatch and jumped out onto the landing pad. Merlin called a question to me, but I did not acknowledge it at the moment.

There was an open door not fifty meters away from the *Freedom*, and fresh air and the scent of warm-blooded mammalian life came in on the breeze. I was outside the door in three heartbeats, and began tracking a rabbit-like creature about the size of a large Terran dog. Its warm blood was exactly what I needed that day. By the time I had returned to port an hour later, the headache was almost completely gone. Luckily for me, I was able to slip into a sanitary cubicle for a little while to clean up before returning to the ship. I was a bit puzzled by my literal craving for fresh blood that day, as I had been doing quite well on synthetics for some time. It particularly concerned me because I knew that synthetics were all that would be available while traveling back to Fleet territory.

Merlin was still close to the *Freedom*, chatting just outside with a young Andree named Loe ker D'een who was often in Port Viste. At my approach, the Andree ducked his head politely toward me and said, "Young Merlin has done well, Honor!"

I cheerfully agreed with him and noticed one more time how tall and adult young Merlin now looked. When close to a child as it grows, it is sometimes difficult to realize when maturity has arrived. Merlin's sleek gray fur enhanced rather than hid the well-defined muscles of his shoulders and legs and gave the impression of great strength and power. It was difficult to believe that he was one of the two tiny kittens I had first seen a mere three years past. Deliberately, I refused to think about Morgana.

Instead I nudged Merlin's ribs gently and said, "Very well done, Merlin-sweetie. Are you up to handling the trip back, as well?"

Arching his long whiskers in pleasure, Merlin was still young enough to envelop me in the equivalent of a bear-hug between those paws as he declared, "Thank-you, Honor! You feel better now, yes?"

"Yes, pussy-cat," I teased. "Come on, let's go greet the security chief and stretch our legs a bit before going back, eh?"

Accompanying me, Merlin remarked, "Loe mentioned to me that there have been incidents with Wolfen ships in this area recently. Ships have been stopped and searched and never informed what it was the Wolfen wanted."

Shrugging, I remarked, "That sounds typical of them." Glancing at his unemotional face, I added, "Don't worry too much about them, sweetie. We'll be fine."

"I'm not concerned about us. Not today, Honor," Merlin replied seriously, "I'm wondering what will happen when we take the *Serpentine* away from Viste and the space controlled by Lord Drakyn's influence." His big paw picked up my hand, at which point he stopped walking, making me turn to face him.

"Honor, they…the Wolfen…murdered my sister," Merlin said intensely.

I was surprised at the comment, as this was the first time he had spoken about it in years.

"I am not afraid for myself, but rather for you, Honor," he continued. "You said that vermin-like creature, Krell, managed to escape that day."

Hoping that the big felinoid could not hear my pulse, as Drakyn invariably did, I met his gaze evenly and replied, "I am not afraid of Krell, or any other Wolfen, Merlin. If I do encounter him, I will take great pleasure in doing my utmost to destroy him myself." The venom behind my words surprised even me.

"If you are outnumbered…," Merlin began, but stopped at my interruption.

"Listen, puss," I said, more than a bit sarcastically, "You are forgetting that I am very much like Lord Drakyn myself. Even outnumbered by the Wolfen, I can do a great deal of damage to them, of that I can assure you!" Then I grinned up at him. "Relax, Merlin! This day is supposed to be fun, remember?"

Shaking his head, Merlin agreed, "Of course, you are right, Honor. I will trust your judgment, as usual."

We did not speak of it again, but I kept remembering the conversation all day, unsure how I felt about it myself.

***

LESS than two solar months later the *Serpentine* was completed, and Gall had contracted the last two members of our crew—a Coryan assistant engineer and a tiny four-legged Diamatay, who Seca assured me was incredible with food processing programs. At last my crew of ten was complete, plus Merlin.

The night before we departed Viste, I spent alone in Drakyn's company in the north tower of the castle. We did not speak of my leaving until the sun was rising over the distant treetops. Drakyn was holding me in his arms as he stood at one of the huge windows. Almost abruptly, he said, "You must take your ship's invisibility device away from Viste with you, Honor. Keep it close to you always."

"But, I'll be back here. Surely you'll keep it safe for me, won't you?" I asked uncomfortably.

He dropped a light kiss on my forehead and simply repeated, "Take it with you, little one. Tell no one about it. Keep it a secret between us."

"Drakyn, I WILL return here!" I assured him. "I can't stay away from you forever! Unless you want me to...?" I lowered my head, looking away from his face, afraid of what I might see there.

"Honor," Drakyn said compellingly, and then his hand raised my face toward his. Those dark-blue eyes were again intense enough to make my knees weak as he stated, "Even if you never choose to return here, I would be compelled to come and seek you out myself. Remember, we are linked—entwined if you will—and whatever you wish me to know of you, how you feel, or what you need, I will always feel and know these things."

Smiling in relief, I nodded. "Of course," I said, adding, "Anything . . . everything, Drakyn," as I had declared to him so long ago.

Somehow, it made it easier for me to leave Viste knowing that Drakyn was not in the port area. Merlin and I traveled up to the *Serpentine* in the small *Freedom* shuttle, and I was rather nostalgic as I recalled how I had come to this place just over four years ago as a vulnerable human prisoner, expecting slavery and worse. Now I was leaving a place that I considered my second home, where I was treated with deference of the kind afforded royalty. I was pleased to be Drakyn's Lady, a protein-drinker, and the captain of my own ship.

The ten solar weeks it took us to return to Fleet space were important weeks of thinking for me. The day I left Viste I really did not know what I was going to do. Somehow, I needed to find a balance between being duty-bound to Fleet Command, and the freedom to take the *Serpentine* out and just explore the possibilities. I had serious doubts about my ability to be content with a return to the commissioned ranks of the Fleet, but it was my duty to do so now, and to make my reports. Some of the information I had learned about the Wolfen would be of great value and interest to Fleet Intelligence. The contract time of my Fleet Service had expired more than a year past, and after filing a report on what happened to me, I would be free to stay or go.

Six solar months after my return to Earth, I knew exactly what I would be doing for the next few years. An old instructor and friend, Admiral Kimitake, now head of Fleet Intelligence, was delighted to recruit me as a private citizen—no longer active military. I would work as an independent operative both inside and outside Fleet controlled space. For that reason, my return to the Fleet had been kept a very close secret. I had no living family, so there was no real reason to reveal the news of my return to anyone. Kimitake was also very helpful in sponsoring Merlin to be accepted to the Fleet Academy, and initial reports assured Kimitake that the young felinoid gave every indication of being a rising star.

Merlin understood how important it was to keep the details of our relationship and of Drakyn's power base on Viste to himself. His instincts were much more mature than his age in years, so I had few worries about him. In the Academy, his unknown racial heritage did not hinder him in the least; the Fleet had a very enlightened policy toward alien life forms during that period of history. Merlin's good nature and disarmingly kind manners earned him friends almost at once. I expected great things in his future.

When I realized that I wanted to spend some time on Earth myself, to investigate what the Fleet wanted from me, I encouraged Gall to begin a freighting route in that particular system—at least for now. I privately assured him that things would change as soon as I had finished my work on Earth. My good and loyal friend did as I suggested, with very few questions and minimal grumbles. During that time, I did not even attempt to send a message to or get a message from Drakyn on Viste. In fact, my reports to the Fleet were deliberately inaccurate as to the exact position of that particular planet, instead stressing that it was on the edge of Wolfen space and absolutely not interested in a Fleet alliance.

I learned much about intelligence operations, and weapons design and use, perfecting my already-enhanced hand-to-hand defenses, and becoming well-versed in the politics between the Fleet and other systems. Most importantly, I managed to keep my new non-human attributes and real powers secret from everyone but Admiral Kimitake, who privately acknowledged how useful I had become to him. When I left Earth again, it was aboard the *Serpentine* with Gall and the crew. I had been honorably discharged from the Fleet and I joined the freight hauling business Gall had begun at my direction. The first thing we did was to put out the word that we were available to haul greater distances, outside the system and into other areas of space.

The exact details of the next several years of my career need not be explored here. Suffice it to say that I was very busy, and the results I provided for Fleet Intelligence were quite useful in maintaining the peace between the greater powers of the galaxy. Politics itself did not interest me much; I primarily concentrated on circumventing whatever plans the Wolfen were developing for conquest or invasion of free space. Thus, I was able to return to Viste, though not to stay. My crew was happy with me, and vice versa, so my visits to Viste were mostly of the "shore leave" variety. Drakyn and I thoroughly enjoyed every moment we spent together, but I never indicated I would remain on Viste, and he did not seem to expect otherwise. Whenever the *Serpentine* left Viste, I always hesitated as I bid Drakyn farewell, feeling on some level that it just might be for the last time.

***

KRELL. I heard his name mentioned repeatedly in conversations about the Wolfen command structure, and I also read his name in reports documenting Wolfen attacks upon Fleet settlements on the outer edges of free space. Informants also whispered Krell's name to me. They believed they were warning a trading captain about a mutual enemy, and I could not disagree with their assessment. Krell was now a Wolfen battle cruiser captain, and his reputation for cunning and ruthlessness was growing greater with every report. He and the crew of the Wolfen battle cruiser, *Revenge*, were particularly likely to launch sudden and devastating raids upon remote Fleet settlements, killing everyone they could locate, and then destroying the settlement.

There were more than a few occasions when I was able to score a minor victory over Krell by alerting the Fleet to his proximity in a certain sector, and they were able to arrive in time to protect settlements in the area. Despite his reputation, and my own experiences with Krell, I realized that my hate for him and what he represented had faded with time. Indeed, I no longer hated him, but by the same token I did not like him either. I respected him in the same way I would respect any poisonous animal.

What happened next, however, was a serious mistake on my part.

I had taken my *Freedom* shuttle out to conduct some side exploration in and around a huge asteroid belt in the Chinella sector of border space. The *Serpentine* had just visited a Fleet port for a period of nearly five weeks while I had the port nacelle re-balanced by Gall and a hand-picked crew of technicians whom Gall had chosen. Three solar weeks out from that port we were again proceeding toward Viste.

For some reason I could not explain, I often prowled the deck of the *Serpentine*'s bridge like an unhappy cat. I knew I was making my crew nervous, so when I encountered an interesting asteroid belt I decided to go out and explore the area for the next solar day. I gave Gall and Seca orders to continue on their set course, stating that I would follow them to Viste in the *Freedom*. This was not unusual for me, and I believed that my crew was probably relieved to see me go off on my own for a while.

The *Freedom* took me deeply into the asteroid belt, and I spent some time maneuvering between the giant rocks while speeding through space, content with my own company. Suddenly I came around a planet-sized asteroid and found myself heading directly for a massive Wolfen battle cruiser. I scarcely had time to cut back the *Freedom*'s power and sharply turn her about before the energy tractors slammed down upon my much smaller ship. With a sinking feeling in my stomach, I realized that this Wolfen ship was actually the *Revenge*!

I was in deep trouble, and hooked like a fish on a line. It did not take *Revenge*'s energy tractors long at all to reel me inside the vessel.

Chapter 12

Piercing Space

DRAKYN stood in his private chamber, staring out the arched window at his view of the pine trees and river below the castle. He knew something was going to occur soon, and the fact that Honor was somewhere unknown did not make him feel any better about his premonitions regarding her. There were still details that he knew were important, yet these remained just beyond his reach and his sense of disquiet made him hesitant to pursue them. Shrugging his wide shoulders, he told himself he ought to work off some of these thoughts with exercise or physical labor. Yet, no matter how vigorously he occupied himself, Honor still haunted his thoughts.

Suddenly he realized that someone had been knocking at his door repeatedly, so he moved away from the window and opened it. He blinked in surprise to see Merlin standing there, his green eyes slit with pleasure as the young felinoid unselfconsciously stepped forward to embrace him in a manner quite absent the usual reserve of his adopted Malkin race.

Drakyn could not keep himself from softening at Merlin's unrestrained affection, and he returned the embrace quickly, saying, "Hello, lad. I had not heard you would be on Viste. It is good to see you!" Then he noticed the new gold bars on the white uniform cuffs that Merlin wore. "You've been promoted, I see. A captain now!"

Ducking his head in humble acknowledgment, Merlin replied, "I assumed my first command of the *Integrity* a solar year past. She is in port undergoing a major refit, and this is my first opportunity to come home. I learned that the *Serpentine* was on its way to Port Viste, so I quickly arranged a ride here to spend some time with the family, you, and Honor. I just saw Gall, and he said that Honor is traveling alone in the *Freedom*. He seems to think she'll arrive any day."

"It's possible," Drakyn acknowledged, smiling slightly at Merlin's ever-optimistic attitude. It occurred to him that his tolerance for the kitten's youthful antics had grown into real affection for the adult Merlin. "Tell me about your ship and your command, lad," he finally said, as he moved with him through the corridor and down the steps toward the great hall where they knew the evening meal would soon be served.

It was not long before Tarquin, Pried ker D'at and others of Drakyn's household appeared. At Drakyn's suggestion, Merlin also contacted Gall and Seca Fordivite and asked them to join the group. Thus, within an hour the hall was filled with warm conversation and laughter, as many adventures and anecdotes were exchanged together with delicious food and wine. As was usual, Drakyn took his tall, throne-like chair at the head of the big table. He was characteristically quiet yet involved in listening carefully to the conversations of the others present. In times past, he would meet with his top managers at similar gatherings, giving orders, gathering information from their experiences, and learning of their concerns. Thus, this sort of event had been a tradition on Viste for many years. Tonight, Drakyn reflected, it provided a sort of continuity between generations as their lives moved beyond this particular family, group, planet and loyalty. It was strangely comforting.

In such relaxed and jovial company, Drakyn was not expecting nor prepared for the cry that rang out sharply in his mind, piercing light years of space. It overtook and enveloped around his thoughts like water surrounds a drowning victim. He was overwhelmed by the experience of its sender. Desperation and the terrible knowledge of what had just occurred, and what was about to happen, made the cry impossible to ignore. Drakyn uttered a short, violent oath. He stood so abruptly that his heavy wooden chair fell over with a crash. Involuntarily, he raised both arms as if to ward off an attacker. Splinters of wood slid over the polished stone floor with enough velocity that slivers were later discovered embedded in the thick tapestry covering a wall more than 10 meters behind him. The faces of his managers all registered various levels of alarm as they stared at him. The visible lengthening of Drakyn's blood teeth made more than one of them seriously consider running from the chamber in an effort to escape the known fury of the dreaded Lord.

For several heartbeats they were all frozen in frightened uncertainty. It was Tarquin who, with his own thick gray mane ruffled up in alarm, finally spoke with deliberate calm. He asked the Lord of Viste how he might serve him.

The great Lord's eyes were unfocussed, looking almost blinded by whatever thought or vision had agitated his mind sufficiently to make him leap up, as if prepared to do battle. The peaceful tone of his lieutenant seemed to bring Drakyn back from whatever painful scene he was experiencing, and he blinked at the big felinoid for a moment before speaking three words in a tone of immeasurable, scarcely controlled, fury: "I must go."

"I will accompany my lord," Tarquin stated at once, moving to his side.

"As will I!" Merlin affirmed strongly.

"Prepare my ship, the *Nobleseed*, immediately," Drakyn commanded, nodding at them. The expression on his handsome face remained haunted and distracted.

"Tell us what has happened, Drakyn!" Merlin urged, voicing something few of the others would have dared. "Where are we going?"

"To my lady," Drakyn returned in a hiss. "To Honor!" Then he turned on his heel and strode from the chamber without a backward glance.

Tarquin heard one of the other Malkin felinoids in the chamber draw a hissing breath and ask aloud, "Has he gone mad? The female is probably in Fleet-controlled space. She works among her own kind!"

It was Pried ker D'at who spoke Tarquin's own thought: "Drakyn and Honor *are* the same kind. No matter if her origins are

Terran humanoid. They are one now. Mated in blood. Something none of us can begin to understand."

Tarquin nodded respectfully toward the Coryan Port Master before he followed Lord Drakyn from the chamber. There was much to accomplish, as quickly as possible.

Merlin remained in the room with the others, his big paws curled into clawed fists. He stared for a long moment at the door where they had exited, and then turned to Gall and Seca Fordivite and said, "Gall, will you assist me?"

The big alien moved close to the felinoid and affirmed gruffly, "In any way, in any manner!"

"Then ready the *Serpentine* as well. Drakyn will take out his ship and I will accompany him. Stay at a distance, but in contact. We will need your backup."

Less than six standard hours later Drakyn sat in the command seat of his most prized and technologically advanced ship, the *Nobleseed*. The ship was not large. It carried only six beings comfortably, and at the moment it held Drakyn, Merlin, and Tarquin. As they left orbit, Tarquin observed that Drakyn was entering navigational coordinates that would take them deep into Wolfen-controlled space. He exchanged a glance with Merlin and then looked silently but pointedly at his son's Fleet uniform cuffs.

The Lord of Viste turned to them then and said abruptly, "Honor has been taken captive by a Wolfen ship captained by Krell, an old enemy. I will free her at any cost. Beings will die. It is my responsibility alone, not that of those who serve me on Viste. You may both transport back to Viste before we are too distant, if you so desire."

Shaking his shaggy head, Tarquin responded immediately, "I have always served and honored you. I wish to accompany you."

Merlin met Drakyn's eyes and got to his feet, peeling off his Fleet command cuffs. He dropped them into a disposal drawer and then nudged it shut with his hip. The sound of a vacuum lock discharge was plainly heard. He knew that this mission could become extremely ugly, and there should be no evidence of any Fleet involvement. It was not necessary for him to speak.

Drakyn accepted their decision with a bow of his head and remained silent as they went through the routine duties required for piloting the ship at extremely accelerated speeds.

It was more than four solar days before Drakyn was able to locate the ship he sought. The *Revenge* had a reputation, even within the areas of space controlled by the Wolfen, and so its whereabouts were typically known. Drakyn had a way of persuading other ships they encountered to provide him with information when it seemed unlikely that they might cooperate. Observing him, Merlin learned much. Drakyn would invariably insist upon a face-to-face meeting to present his request for information, and it was soon plain to his companions that no one could resist the power of Drakyn's persuasive will.

Once Drakyn managed to obtain the identification markings of the *Revenge*, he would hunt the ship until he located it. After several solar days Tarquin asked a question that was plaguing his mind, "My lord, the *Revenge* is a battle-class star ship, carrying a complement of more than one hundred troopers. The *Nobleseed* carries only us three. How can we presume to engage such a large ship and not expect to be destroyed?"

Drakyn glanced up from the navigation boards that so obsessed his attention during the trip, but stated only, "By the time we reach the *Revenge*, most of the crew will have been killed. If you put your trust in me, I will now share my plans with you."

Tarquin was silent, but he could feel his fur ruffling up on the back of his neck. He looked over at his adopted son and could see that the words had a similarly chilling effect on him, despite the excitement and determination he also saw in Merlin's eyes.

Chapter 13

Insanity

CAPTIVITY does not agree with me at all. I don't make a good prisoner, hostage, slave, or servant. Force and coercion bring out the worst side of my nature, as future histories will confirm, but I am getting ahead of myself.

When I was captured by the Wolfen, I seriously considered implementing the self-destruct mechanism of the ship before they were able to pry it open and get me out of the craft. It would have been quite satisfying to blow out their shuttle bay and probably explode the entire battleship, or a good portion of it, rather than letting Krell take me into custody. However, such an action would have inevitably killed or permanently maimed me as well as the Wolfen, and I was not prepared to surrender to that just yet. I suspect it can be considered a cowardly character flaw in me, but I wanted to remain in one physical piece for some time longer.

In truth, I also had to admit that I had become arrogant and self-assured enough to think that I just might find a way to escape, even while learning something useful about the Wolfen in the process. All of these thoughts were churning through my head as I sat with a power weapon trained upon the *Freedom*'s interior hatch door, listening to the Wolfen crew outside as they prepared to blast their way inside. In a belated flash of insight, I suddenly realized that I had better just open the hatch rather than allow them to destroy any portion of my little ship in their anxious efforts to get inside. So at the last possible moment I opened the hatch myself, threw out my power weapon, and emerged with a gesture of surrender.

Krell awaited me there, looking quite pleased with himself, and accompanied by no less than ten of his troopers. All of them had their weapons aimed at me. It took a real effort on my part to keep from laughing aloud at their serious intent to blow a single female humanoid into tiny pieces if a wrong move was made.

Instead, I focused intensely upon the Wolfen captain and managed to actually smile at him. Then, with all of the mental power at my command I said, "It's been a long time, Krell! I understand you've been looking for me?"

Needless to say Krell was not amused by my opening gambit, and I was quickly dragged away from the shuttle bay to a dim, metal-walled cube that served as my cell for some time. Its only furnishings were a pull-down bunk and a sanitary unit that functioned only sporadically. Facilities engineering was apparently not as highly regarded among the Wolfen fleet as it seemed to be among other space traveling races. It seemed likely to me that a female in my position aboard a Wolfen ship had good reason to worry about sexual assault in this situation. It was also plain from the first moment that Krell wanted to get at me. He desired more than a simple opportunity to pay me back for what had occurred so many years before on planet Viste.

Surprisingly, that first day, when he pushed me against my own ship and put a claw-like hand under my tunic, his own crewmembers dragged him away from me furiously. They had horrified expressions on their dark faces and traced symbols around themselves as if for protection. I had learned enough of their language over the years to understand their concerns. They were afraid that Krell was dooming their ship to destruction by sexually assaulting a female aboard it. This taboo had not been revealed in any information provided to me during my Fleet training. Lucky for me they had such an aversion. I silently hoped that Krell did not decide to make a stop at some planetoid and transport me down to the surface so he could rape me.

Instead, Krell diverted his sexual frustration by having me interrogated every few hours, while personally lurking only a short physical distance from me. I will not waste time detailing the kinds of interrogation techniques the Wolfen used. Krell had several very skilled practitioners in that particular field and they spared me very little, from threats to pain. They also attempted to use drugs to break down my will and make me surrender emotionally to them. However, although they sometimes clouded my mind, I seemed rather immune to their chemicals.

It actually took me some time to puzzle out exactly what they wanted to learn from me. Only when Krell began shouting at me in a fit of temper did I realize that it was not political secrets they sought. Krell and his people honestly believed that I was truly a female pirate captain, as I had been pretending for some time. Krell wanted the details of the "power" I had. Over the years he had made a point of learning everything he could about me, just as Chivv R had long-ago warned me. He also desired information about Lord Drakyn's strengths and weaknesses on Viste.

Krell knew I was a blood drinker. He had learned of it years ago, and had seen how I drained the blood from his captain on Viste. Thus, he was frightened by the power I invoked, both physically and emotionally, when pushed beyond control. It was plain to me from the start that he wanted to tap into its source, perhaps by pushing me to the limits of my tolerance. He kept his intentions a secret, even from his own staff, ordering them only vaguely to interrogate me, examine me, and torment me into surrendering my "secrets" to them. After a few days, he instructed his medical staff to begin drawing samples of my blood for analysis. He demanded that they explain the kind of physical power I would involuntarily demonstrate when I was pushed beyond any kind of patience.

I never even pretended not to know what he wanted.

During this time I did not just cower back and allow these creatures to hurt me; I fought back rather effectively, at first. Twice I managed to overcome my guards and escape my cell, only to be thwarted in my attempts to reach my shuttle craft. Once I was able to get a medical technician to look me directly in the eye, and then managed to persuade his impressionable mind that it was imperative to get me off of the *Revenge* before the vast power of the Fleet attacked and destroyed them all. My control over that fellow never wavered, even as we fought off Krell and six others.

Eventually, however, they killed their own crewman and I was again overcome.

Perhaps I should have felt guilty about that fellow's death, but I did not. He had been drugging me and causing me pain. After that incident, however, Krell did not allow any of the crew members to be entirely alone with me. The Wolfen might be a bit slow, but they did learn eventually what might hurt them.

The blood analysis worried me, especially when they kept returning to me and taking more and more blood for examination. Of course I did not like it—no sane person would—but it worried me mostly because it was weakening me. I also suspected that they might discover something that even I could not hide.

Krell had ordered that I was to be provided with fruits and vegetable matter for sustenance, but absolutely no protein, natural or synthesized. Thus, the food they allowed me provided absolutely no nutrition for my protein-dependent systems, and the regular withdrawal of blood samples weakened me further. Within days it was an effort to even stand on my own. I took refuge within myself, doing my best to tune out my surroundings, while trying desperately to think of a way to save myself and to remain alert enough not to miss any opportunity to take action.

Several days after my capture, during a night watch, Krell came into my cell alone. He closed the portal after himself and stood leaning against it staring at me. I had been dozing on my cot, conserving my energy. When I saw that he was there alone I strongly suspected that no one else knew he was present. The crew seemed to vigilantly guard their captain against his own inclinations, but he must have evaded them this time. He stepped toward me suddenly, and my heart began pounding as adrenaline kicked in and warned me to pay strict attention to him.

I blinked for a moment at the clear vial he held out toward me. It contained a vivid red liquid.

Krell's rough tones whispered: "It's pure synthetic protein. Do you want it?"

"At what price?" I asked softly.

"You have a suspicious nature," Krell replied, holding the vial up toward a light source. "Perhaps I am concerned that you have become too weak to survive further questioning."

"Right," I agreed sarcastically. "What do you really want?"

I was surprised when he said, "An alliance with you, Honor. I know that you obtained your powers from the being they call Lord Drakyn on Viste. Physically, you are far stronger than any humanoid female of several races. You have demonstrated strategic talent as well. Share those powers with me. Ally with me and we will be an irresistible force. You are interested in profit; your pirating activities confirm that. If we combined our efforts, any ship we encounter would bow to us."

I snatched the vial from his extended hand, and was surprised that he did not try to take it back from me. When I met his gaze his eyes seemed to burn with some kind of fire that was not sexual. His next words opened a window in my mind, and I suddenly knew what he really wanted from me: "We first encountered each other more than twelve solar years ago, Honor. You have not aged at all."

In some circles such a remark might have been taken as polite conversation. Coming from Krell, however, it revealed everything to me. In those years, Krell had already aged considerably, as was normal with his short-lived race, while I had not changed in any visible manner. It was common knowledge on and around planet Viste that Drakyn had ruled for more than a century without any sign of aging. Krell had observed a similar proclivity in me—a female that he knew for a fact had originated among Terran humans, and who should have grown visibly older during this same period of time.

Age was slowing Krell down now, and he wanted, more than any other achievement or victories, to find a way to keep himself physically young. Any extra powers I could provide him would only be a plus. Keeping my face from showing my thoughts, I replied in a light tone, "The Wolfen race ages quickly, Krell. Mine is slower." I opened the vial and sniffed it cautiously. There was no obvious sign of poison or drugs, but I hesitated nevertheless and closed the vial again.

"You're Terran human," Krell stated. "The DNA scans confirmed this. You should have aged significantly in twelve standard years! Stop playing games with me, Honor. You can give me what I want."

"Of course I can," I agreed with him, adding, "but I won't."

Krell unfolded his arms and took an aggressive step toward

me, hissing, "You are not being given a choice!" He came close enough to touch me, but did not. "I have been careful, even gentle with you thus far. I can force that information from you, female… among other things…!"

His claw-like hand closed around my right wrist, tightening his grip until I dropped the vial to the deck. Then he pushed his big body against mine. Clearly his intentions were shifting to something else now.

We were alone in the cabin. I had no other options, so I slid my free hand up along his leather-clad chest toward his throat, calculating my chances at overcoming him and getting out of this cell. Knowing that I was in danger and knowing how the Wolfen approached females, I should not have been surprised when he struck the first blow. His rough hand caught me just under the left side of my jaw and I was thrown backward against the bulkhead hard enough to stun me for a moment. Perhaps I should have drunk that protein at my first opportunity; it might have given me more strength to physically battle him.

A Terran or Coryan male would have been easy for me to repel, even in a weakened state, but a Wolfen was another matter entirely. He took no chances. He kicked my ribs while I struggled to get back up, and then grasped the front of my already-damaged tunic and ripped it half off of me as he pulled me back to my feet.

"I am the master here," he murmured hoarsely before he punched me in the stomach, keeping a strong hand on my shoulder to prevent me from falling again.

While I was still retching helplessly, Krell turned me around and forced me face-down across the bunk and ripped at my clothing. He mounted me immediately, roughly, and took his damned time satisfying himself. He had twisted one of my arms backward and up behind my back. Among other things, I felt my shoulder dislocate during his growling thrusts. Furious and frightened by my helplessness, my brain screamed out to Drakyn in a way I have never done in the past. I lost consciousness for a brief time while Krell was busy painfully demonstrating his male superiority upon my body.

When I regained my senses it was to the renewed pain of claw-like hands manipulating my damaged shoulder back into its socket. I was unable to keep from screaming slightly as the joint popped back into place. I did not, could not, open my eyes just yet. My mind was struggling to retain its sanity.

"Your arm and hand will be useless for a time," said a voice I recognized as one of the medical staff that had interrogated me with drugs—a Wolfen physician named Bersunn. "Krell wanted to leave your shoulder as it was, but I pointed out that it might make the others more suspicious than they already are."

My eyes snapped open when I felt a warm and wet cloth being drawn over my completely exposed body. He was washing me like an infant or an invalid.

Bersunn's alien eyes were impersonal when I met them, and he was smart enough to look away quickly. "Krell has forbidden pain blocks for you. He said you'd heal yourself quickly enough. The scan does not indicate internal bleeding, despite the discoloration on your belly." He picked up a pale gray garment of the sort worn in a sick bay or hospital. "Are you able to sit up and get into this clothing?"

It took an effort, and eventually his assistance, but I managed to sit upright on the bunk with every muscle in my arm and shoulder screaming in protest. I took a deep breath to fight nausea and immediately realized that I probably had a cracked rib or two as well. Bersunn put the long tunic over me and helped me get my arms into it. Then he sealed the tabs down my back. It was big enough that it fit me like a knee-length gown.

As he did so, I caught his eyes with my own again and said: "You know what Krell did, don't you?"

Inclining his head slightly, the Wolfen physician replied, "I do not approve of his actions, but I am not gullible. He is my commander. I can assure you of one thing: If you speak of what Krell did before any other crew member, Krell will cut out your tongue and no one will stop him. Then the only thing that might absolve this crew of Krell's crime will be your death. These people are most superstitious."

Not trusting my voice, I kept silent.

Bersunn stepped back from me now and advised, "You should sleep now, while you can. Krell has ordered that your blood be drained to bring you as close to death as possible, beginning during first morning watch. He wants great quantities of your blood." He paused and picked something up from the deck and then dropped the vial of red liquid into my lap. "For your own sake," he said, "drink this now." Then he left me.

At first I did not move at all. My right hand was still numb and useless. It took me a few heartbeats of time to do it, but I used my left hand to open the vial and bring it to my lips. At that moment, I did not even care if it was drugged or poisoned. It was not. The pure protein flooded my starving systems immediately, and I could feel the strength returning to my limbs like circulation in my veins. The thoughts in my brain suddenly became very clear. I was blood of Drakyn's blood; I was a formidable force. I was a valuable agent for Fleet Intelligence. I had value as an individual, no matter whatever had occurred here in this cabin. Krell would be made to pay for this attack, somehow, somewhere. Lying back, I willed myself toward uneasy, painful sleep. Dreams of pain, humiliation, and a desire for violent retribution were my companions.

When the medical staff came for me hours later, I was immediately put on an examination table and rolled to the ship's medical section. There, my arms and legs were strapped down with belts that I probably could have broken if I had been at full strength. It was difficult to remain fully awake for some reason, but the sound of Krell's rough voice close by brought me back to complete attention.

"Ah, good, you're back with us, Honor," Krell's tones sneered at me in false joviality. "I did not wish you to miss this party!" He leaned over me, leering at my chest that was half exposed by the deep V in the tunic designed for male physiques. When I did not bother to reply, he remarked pointedly, "You are looking paler than ever, Honor. Thinner. I suspect you are not enjoying my hospitality. A pity."

I was thinking about how thirsty I was at the moment, and how the scent of Wolfen male only added to my need for fresh blood, and how even Krell's would have served the purpose.

Yet when he leaned even closer to me, his rank breath made me remember what he had done, and my stomach curled up under my ribs. I opened my mouth to breathe through it and fight off the nausea. Suddenly, Krell's claw-like hand caught hold of my chin and then forced my mouth open even wider.

"See her fangs?" Krell exulted to the others in the room. "She's a hungry bitch now, and wants to tear out my throat, and then the throat of everyone else aboard, don't you, Honor? A pity you won't be given the opportunity! Tap her veins. Now!"

One of the medical staff came near with a blade and sliced deeply into the visible vein of my immobilized right wrist, and then the left. Following this, he inserted thin tubes. The pain was minimal, but the alarm flooding my brain was overwhelming me. Turning my head, I could see that they had placed bottle-like containers beneath my wrists and they were gathering the blood into them. A moment later the medical assistant similarly tapped the veins in both of my ankles. There was nothing I could do about it.

"She will drain and probably die quickly now," Bersunn predicted solemnly, a little frown on his face.

I blinked at him in surprise; I had not realized he was present.

"Do not allow that. I don't want her dead. Have the stasis unit ready to take her body when she reaches a critical point," Krell directed confidently. "We'll keep her alive and harmless until we reach our home world where we can present her to the Pack Leaders. Until that time, I will nourish myself with her blood to become just as powerful as this female, yet enhanced by my Wolfen physical advantages." Still holding a hand over my mouth and jaw, Krell leaned over and bit deeply into the flesh of my inner thigh.

I shouted out in surprise and pain; I could scarcely move as his sharp teeth fastened upon my flesh and began to suck my blood into his mouth. The clawed hand on my chin slipped just slightly and I took the opportunity to bite him viciously, enough to draw a mouthful of blood from him before he ripped his hand away from my mouth with a curse. The bitter Wolfen blood was very protein-rich and I was overwhelmed with a craving for more of it immediately. The need actually blurred my vision as I glanced at my right wrist and literally ripped it free of the belt securing it.

Krell might have noticed my actions, but he was far too engrossed in his own activities. I endured a second laceration of my leg by his craggy teeth, and again felt him sucking blood from the wound.

My right hand was now free of the restraint, but I did not have the strength to release the other wrist yet. I pretended not to be quite as alert as the taste of Krell's blood had made me. I then placed my hand over the collection bottle and managed to slow the flow of blood into it. I knew this would cause Bersunn to come and investigate, making him move closer to me again. The sound of Krell's slurping noises and the disgusting feel of his mouth on my leg was a bit distracting. Time was very short; I had to move before the blood Krell was taking from me began to affect his brain.

Krell had come to the conclusion that simply drinking my blood would give him my power. He was very, very wrong. What it would do was make him dangerously and violently insane. Drakyn had warned me about this sort of danger long ago and I trusted his word without ever testing it.

Bersunn came closer to me again, adjusting the bottle beneath my still secured, left wrist. I expected he would lean over me to check my eyes in a moment. When he did not, I opened my eyes in time to see the foolish Wolfen medical doctor upend the bottle of my blood into *his* own mouth! Clearly, Krell had shared his ideas with Bersunn, who also wanted whatever power Krell was expecting. I reached up and dragged Bersunn down to my own mouth without so much as a squeak from him. My blood teeth sliced into his scaly throat and I inhaled his alien blood like it was the best possible vintage wine. The effect upon my strength was immediate. In the same moment that I felt Krell raise his mouth from my leg, I broke the rest of my bonds. I bucked both Wolfen warriors away from me, tore out the tubes, slipped off the table, and landed on my feet before either could react.

While I quickly scanned the chamber for an escape path, the door behind Krell and Bersunn slid open and another medical officer entered. His eyes quickly fixed on me, concerned only that a prisoner was attempting escape again.

Krell fell upon the unsuspecting officer and ripped open his throat with his claws before pressing his mouth to the gaping wound. The physician, with my blood still on his mouth, shakily pulled himself to his feet and stared at Krell's actions for a moment and then joined him in draining the newcomer.

Restraining a near-hysterical urge to laugh at them, I slipped around the dangerous fools and got out before they decided to harvest any more of my blood.

Krell and the medical officer would be insane until their bodies completely absorbed and then eliminated my protein-dependent blood. They would be wild animals until that occurred, for hours, maybe even longer. The damage to the rest of the *Revenge*'s crew would be horrific. It would be best if I got off this ship now. If that was not possible, I had better find a good place to hide!

I realized that my wounds were still leaking drops of blood, so I pushed myself into an alcove and turned my attention to each of my lacerations, commanding them to heal over. It still surprised me when that actually happened as I willed it. Then I tried to do the same thing with the muscles and tendons surrounding my shoulder. However, I soon realized that I needed more protein to get anywhere. I had consumed more than enough Wolfen blood for now, so I would try to find something synthetic. More clothing would also make things even better, at least as far as my confidence was concerned.

After that, I needed a safe place to hide for a while.

Chapter 14

Bloody Vessel

THE readings from the Wolfen ship were nearly silent, except for the soft clicks and murmurs generated by its navigational computer. The vessel's automated systems seemed to be independently conducting the business of maintaining life support and orbital integrity around the uninhabited, medium-sized planetoid which the *Revenge* now circled.

The *Nobleseed* assumed a similar orbit at a distance just beyond the Wolfen ship's scanner range. At Drakyn's side, Merlin's eyes scanned the display boards before them, unsure exactly what the silence meant. When he glanced sidewise at Drakyn, the Lord's face was shuttered from any kind of emotion—not unusual for him, but quite frustrating for those around him. Merlin was bursting with questions about this situation, yet he knew Drakyn well enough to understand that answers would be forthcoming only if the Lord was so inclined.

"Are they all dead?" Merlin finally asked, unable to restrain himself any longer.

"Not yet," was the laconic reply from his elder companion. Then Drakyn startled him by adding, "I have not located Honor's trace yet. Continue scanning. Adjust the gain to 110% of maximum and you will be able to see the individual life traces."

Responding as directed, Merlin immediately began to observe

life traces throughout the ship. In doing so, he felt as if he was able to release a breath held much too long in suspense. "What's happened to them?" he suddenly asked. "A ship this size should have at least one hundred troopers aboard it. I'm scanning no more than twenty here. Wolfen life traces don't usually need to be read at such an intense frequency, and they aren't moving around much right now. Something unusual has occurred aboard that ship!"

"That is entirely true," Drakyn responded, frowning. He paused, as if considering his next move.

"Has whatever happened to them also affected Honor's readings?" Tarquin asked from his position behind them.

"I don't know. They all look pretty much the same—" Merlin began to reply but stopped abruptly when Drakyn reached forward and tapped a particular trace on the screen.

"That is Honor," Drakyn stated. "Before you question me, I can assure you, I know her reading when I see it. See? She is separated from the rest of them and is completely stationary, perhaps unconscious or injured."

"We must go to her," Merlin began.

Drakyn's hand restrained him easily. "Caution, young one. Discretion. Remember your tactical training, lad."

"How can you be so calm about it?" Merlin demanded.

Drakyn looked into Merlin's eyes and the young felinoid was alarmed by the expression that smoldered there. "My calm is merely on the surface, I assure you," he said. Then he suddenly stood up and announced, "I will go aboard that ship alone."

"It could be a trap!" Merlin pointed out.

"I do not believe so," Drakyn said quietly as he opened a bin and took out a sidearm and its holster.

Merlin could not help but cast a glance at Tarquin, and his father's look registered the same surprise he was feeling. Neither of them had ever seen Drakyn touch any hand weapon other than his sword. The power of his mind, his voice, and ultimately his strong hands were usually more than enough weapons on Viste.

"I will go with you," Merlin began again, but stopped short when Drakyn turned toward him sharply with an angry, halting gesture.

"No," Drakyn declared in a final-sounding tone. "You and

Tarquin will remain here."

Not happy about Drakyn's directive, Merlin struggled to continue scanning the monitors as Drakyn used the molecular transporter to go over to the Wolfen ship. He also wore a transporter retrieval wrist band so he could return to the *Nobleseed* when he chose to do so. Merlin knew that Drakyn's very willingness to use the transport device he usually disdained was a signal of how seriously he approached this encounter with whoever remained alive aboard that ship.

The prohibition against any challenge to Drakyn's authority had been trained into Merlin from his earliest memories. However, as a Fleet captain it made him impatient and angry. He had come here to take action, not to sit impotent and helpless, like an adolescent. As soon as Drakyn's trace readings indicated a successful transport had been achieved, Merlin began to punch in his own statistical information, ignoring the outraged snarl from Tarquin beside him. He got to his feet and said calmly, "I didn't come along just to watch, Tarquin. I will go over as well."

Tarquin's large paw grasped hold of Merlin's sleeve and shook him once, strongly. "Do not disobey Lord Drakyn!" he hissed sharply.

"I will allow him one hour of time. After that, I'm taking my chances," Merlin replied evenly. "Drakyn is only one being, no matter how powerful he is, and he will require back-up!"

Tarquin stated, "Drakyn will be furious!"

Arching his whiskers upward, Merlin answered, "Yes, he probably will. Humans have a saying for this: "Too bad!"

During the hour they waited, Tarquin used every kind of persuasion possible to dissuade Merlin from leaving the *Nobleseed*—from reminders of Lord Drakyn's capabilities, to dire warnings about his anger when disobeyed. Finally he lapsed into invoking parental authority to forbid Merlin from going over to the Wolfen ship. Through all of this, Merlin calmly and repeatedly pointed out to Tarquin how utterly strange it was not to observe any kind of movement aboard the Wolfen ship. They knew that Drakyn's trace was shielded from their sensing devices, but the traces they could monitor moved around very little.

Merlin was eventually so persuasive that when he activated the transporter to go over to the Wolfen ship an hour later, his foster father accompanied him, prepared to do battle with whatever they found.

The transporter field would affect their eyesight, hearing, and smell for a few moments following their arrival, and it was during these moments that Merlin knew they would be most vulnerable. For this reason he had taken care to have them materialize in an area where there were no visible life traces—which was, surprisingly, on the ship's main bridge. As their senses cleared, they turned about to survey the dimly-lit area. It was then that Merlin drew in a deep breath, intending to ask Tarquin if he was all right. Suddenly he felt as if he was choking or suffocating, and then made violently ill by some unexpected gaseous atmosphere that their sensors had failed to detect. Merlin felt bile fighting its way up his throat, and he staggered in spite of himself.

His foreleg was quickly supported by Tarquin's muscular paw and a small breathing unit was immediately pulled from his hip pack. In a heartbeat's time it was secured over Merlin's outraged olfactory organ, and he was able to resist the urge to be sick. Blinking in surprise at his apparently unaffected parent, Merlin gratefully drew in a breath of clean oxygen and regained control.

Tarquin arched his whiskers at Merlin and murmured gruffly, "It's obvious that you have little experience with hand-to-hand battling, lad. Your Fleet fights only from a distance in space. This is the kind of thing that happens when warriors kill each other with tooth and claw." He then gestured back toward the center of the chamber, remarking, "It is always disgusting."

Embarrassed by his weakness, no matter how short-lived, Merlin looked in the indicated direction. When he realized what he was looking at, a shocked oath fell from his lips.

The bridge chamber was normally manned by no less than ten Wolfen warriors. There were twelve dead bodies present, three of them still at their posts. Others were sprawled upon the deck beside their chairs. A glance down at his sensing device assured Merlin that all in this chamber were deceased. Massive quantities of spilled purple Wolfen blood stained many of the work pads, and had been splashed liberally upon the walls. More blood was also pooled under each body, running away in little rivulets toward the lowest point in the chamber. The terrible stench that had first greeted them was emanating from the torn out throats, slashed bodies, and Wolfen blood spattered liberally around the bridge.

"This happened days past, perhaps two or three," Tarquin remarked. "The Wolfen keep it warm and humid in their ships. That's what contributed to the stench. I'm sure Drakyn was impressed. I wonder if he found who did it yet. Are you all right, lad?"

Nodding, because he did not trust his voice, Merlin leaned close to one of the bodies to examine it further. He remained near it for only a moment, but then drew back because the smell was permeating his filter. "Let's move out of here," he finally said, heading toward the open portal. He paused and scanned before he exited into the corridor, adding, "Let's find Honor."

"That's Lord Drakyn's job," Tarquin pointed out. "He won't like us being here."

"I don't care!" Merlin countered, frowning down at his sensing device. "Tarquin, is that the reading Drakyn said was Honor's?"

"It is," the older felinoid affirmed.

"It's moving now. So we shall also move," Merlin declared, gesturing toward a far corridor.

He had already taken ten steps in that direction when he realized that he did not hear Tarquin's soft tread behind him. Pausing, he turned just in time to be spattered with his foster father's warm blood.

Chapter 15

Deception

THE hours and days following my escape from Krell's blood-draining experiment had been a series of horror scenes. Krell and the medical doctor, Bersunn, had gone upon an absolute killing spree among the crew. They slew and drained nearly one-third of the population of the ship before they began to regain any control over themselves, some twelve to fourteen hours later.

I had managed to keep out of sight by actually climbing into one of the stasis units they intended to use on me. It was possible to shelter myself there during those first terrible hours, slipping out periodically only for food and water. During one foray I managed to find a clothing synthesizer that produced a one-piece suit and boots, as well as a food server that produced synthetic protein for nourishment. Not wanting to face any crazed Wolfen blood drinkers until I had regained my own strength, I hustled back to the stasis unit to hide and consume the protein.

Even during those short excursions into the corridors, I had seen enough murdered Wolfen soldiers to shock even the most hardened war veteran. These creatures were my enemies, but one could only witness so much bloody death without dreaming of such sights for months and years to come. I knew I would require outside assistance to escape this ship in one piece, and I also knew that Drakyn was already on his way here. I had never actually called out through space for Drakyn's help before, but I sensed that my situation was clear to him. As he drew closer, I began to wonder what possible new horrors I had summoned to release upon this ship. In my solitude and self-counsel I began to feel almost guilty about the kind of actions Drakyn might take when he came here to help me.

Then, some twenty-four hours after my original escape from Krell's control, I witnessed something else Krell was doing. I was moving along the upper air duct pipes over the main assembly hall of the *Revenge*, when I saw Krell addressing a large group of the crew members on the subject of the terrible, bloody murders that were decimating the crew.

I became as still as the pipes and conduits surrounding me as I watched and listened.

Krell paced constantly, and his gestures more abrupt than the rather graceful natural stealth common to Wolfen warrior predators. Although it was not possible to see his eyes from my vantage point above them, I suspected that his eyes continued to hold the unfocussed expression of one who had overindulged in liquor or pleasure drugs. Krell was still half-crazed in the power rush he had experienced from imbibing my undiluted blood. However, he had regained enough control over himself to keep from rushing at everyone he encountered and tearing out their throats. Certainly he did not yet know that he and Bersunn were deluded about having gained some measure of my power.

He spoke in a sharp staccato, unlike his usual tones. "You have all been witness to the terrible murders taking place among us," he began, gesturing to someone to move up close to his side. "The humanoid female is a ravening beast among us, and she must be recaptured and confined at all costs!"

Bersunn moved out of the crowd, still staggering slightly from his own reaction to my blood in his system. At a further gesture from Krell, he pulled back the throat of his tunic and showed the assembled crew members the livid bite mark upon his throat. The wounds looked angry and still bled sluggishly. They should have sealed by now, so I suspected that Bersunn and Krell had deliberately enhanced the bite to make their point.

Bersunn added his voice to the discussion, saying, "Our energy weapons are unlikely to work upon such a creature. It will be far more effective to trap her and then find a way to put her into stasis, whereupon we can take her to our home world to be studied!"

"The female called Honor is not the only creature like this," Krell added in a loud, clear voice. "That despised Lord of Viste made her in his own image. We must find a method to destroy the female and then we can destroy Drakyn and gain control of Port Viste and the wealth it controls!" He paused, allowing the crew time to respond to his comments. Their voices quickly became a chant in the Wolfen language that seemed completely supportive of Krell and his intentions. The deluded fools were admirably loyal to the monster who led them.

Krell then dismissed all of those in attendance, with the exception of his surviving officers, numbering approximately ten individuals. These warriors followed Krell and Bersunn down a corridor to what appeared to be some kind of conference room.

As quietly as I was able, I scurried along the pipelines until I was directly above this chamber. It was relatively easy to silently lift up a corner of the overhead tiles and observe what occurred below me.

Once more Krell was addressing the group, but now he spoke of power and how to gain it. He talked of luxuriating in its warmth, and wielding it to dole out life or death, thereby to effectively become godlike. As he spoke his agitation grew, and I became concerned that he and Bersunn would again launch into this group of officers and start tearing out more throats. However, I then saw what Bersunn was doing—he was filling small metal cups with a red liquid that I scented immediately as my own blood!

It would make me appear quite virtuous if I could report here that I ripped up the tile and shouted out a warning to those Wolfen fools. To do so, however, would be a lie. I did nothing to stop them from drinking that blood. As far as I was concerned, at that moment I was at war with the entire crew of the *Revenge*, and the best way to assure my victory was to allow them to kill each other.

They certainly did just that. The twelve blood-crazed officers proceeded to murder most of the remaining crew during the next thirty-plus hours, while I kept myself out of sight, but busy. I was examining their ship's computer defense systems, looking for a way to destroy the *Revenge*.

I figured twelve-to-one odds were pretty good for me.

Chapter 16

Fools

DRAKYN moved through the Wolfen ship cloaked in a shroud of absolute silence and stealth, the maintenance of which required his complete concentration. The sort of control he wielded over his immediate environment was so extensive that it was possible for him to actually drop something heavy onto a solid deck without any perceivable sound reaching anyone nearby.

Within moments of his appearance upon the *Revenge*, he came face to face with a blood-streaked Wolfen warrior wearing the marks of a lesser officer. The creature was half-mad, actually frothing a pinkish-purple combination of saliva and blood. Drakyn reached out and caught him by his scaly throat. It required scarcely a twist of Drakyn's wrist and the Wolfen warrior was dead, discarded, and disregarded. It had not even occurred to Drakyn that he might interrogate the Wolfen as to Honor's location or her condition. It was not necessary, as Drakyn could feel Honor somewhere nearby, alert and concentrating on something other than an escape. One part of her psyche was holding strict control of her emotions, while the other part seemed to be almost enjoying what she was now doing. This elicited some small amount of concerned puzzlement from the Lord of Viste.

Having moved far enough away from the recently deceased Wolfen officer, Drakyn redirected his concentration and sent a mental push in Honor's direction, ordering her to reply to him immediately. The amusement he sensed now became absolute mirth, and Drakyn wondered if she had reached her mental breaking point by what she had endured and witnessed on this ship. Surely hysteria was to be expected.

And then he clearly heard Honor's "voice" inside his brain, saying with a projected chuckle, "Hysteria is for women in old Victorian novels, Drakyn. My amusement comes from how foolish Krell and his crew are...and from knowing how much fun it will be to kick their collective asses. Now, sweetie, I have figured out how to tap into this ship's main power commands!"

"Come to me," he demanded. "Let me protect you now."

Contrary as always, she responded, "Really, Drakyn, that's on a par with 'look into my eyes,' don't you think? Thank you for coming when I cried out, but please just calm down for a few more ticks while I finish up..!"

"Honor, you're blocking me from your mind!"

"Yes, I know. Aren't you proud of me?"

"Honor...!"

"Drakyn, darling, don't be grumpy. After all, you are the one who insisted I learn how to block thoughts!" Her mental tones were a mocking purr.

Drakyn forced himself to be patient and then stopped at a wall schematic showing the corridor layout of the *Revenge*. He knew ships well enough to identify the general area where the Engineering Section was located, and then went in that direction, certain that Honor would be nearby.

However, before he reached the area he sought, Drakyn came upon a barrier that had been built in the main corridor. It was a recently-erected wall completely blocking the hall in width and height. Work was still being completed on this barrier by disheveled and blood-stained Wolfen warriors. Insanely, they were constructing this wall using the tangled bodies of their murdered shipmates as building materials. Such a sight was appalling enough that even a being as powerful and controlled as Drakyn was forced to pause and stare at it for several heartbeats. Standing in plain sight, not twenty meters from the Wolfen troopers, Drakyn watched as one of the mad ones occasionally paused to bite into a torn throat, sucking at the wound and pulling at the flesh like a starving young animal trying to force milk from a dry teat. They were far too intent upon their actions to notice his presence there, and he did nothing to announce himself.

Drakyn turned away into a side corridor, disgusted. His mind was flooded with memories from his distant past on old Earth. This particular sort of madness had run like wildfire through a mountain village during two terrible days. When it was over, no one—not a man, woman or child—was left alive. It had become his personal duty to destroy those murderers.

Drakyn knew Krell and his officers had initiated this present carnage by drinking Honor's blood.

Pausing, Drakyn considered for a moment how he might proceed. At that instant a door slid open a few steps behind him and he quickly flattened against the bulkhead to see who might emerge. A heartbeat later a Wolfen crewperson stepped into the corridor. He carried a tray of blood samples in one hand, and the markings on his blood-smeared uniform indicated that he had a medical assignment of some kind.

Drakyn caught the fellow by the throat and lifted him off his feet, ignoring the sample tray as it crashed to the deck, shattering vials and splattering blood. The fellow was unable to make a sound. Drakyn glared at him for a moment and then realized that he could detect Honor's scent upon this Wolfen. The scent did not come from the discarded blood samples, but it originated from the Wolfen's sour breath and from the stains upon his clothing.

In a piercing whisper, Drakyn said, "You enjoy drinking helpless blood, do you? So do I!"

Drakyn demonstrated his own technique in vein tapping, with a little twist that should make the fellow useful later.

A sound, very faint and distant, suddenly drew Drakyn's attention upward. He stared overhead for a few seconds and then reached up and pushed his strong hand through the relatively thin materials of the corridor ceiling. Within moments he had hoisted himself up and into the maze of catwalks, cables, conduits, and pipes that encased that ship's communications, environmental controls, and weapons systems. Drakyn sensed that this was where he would locate Honor. It became apparent to him at once that his large size might prove to be a challenge in this cramped space. He chose to discard his long, black cloak and began to climb steadily, silently moving in the direction of Engineering.

***

HONOR was pleased with herself, despite the serious situation in which she was embroiled. The *Revenge's* defense systems had been surprisingly simple to analyze, penetrate, and revise to her own advantage. It occurred to her that she might have been a bit unwise in calling for Drakyn for assistance so desperately, but she reminded herself she had been pushed to her breaking point when she did call out to him. A quiet voice of reason warned her not to get over-confident about her own capabilities, as this could lead to carelessness and disaster.

When she first realized that Drakyn was aboard the ship, her initial desire had been to run to his arms and surrender control of the situation to him. However, she immediately knew that despite how comforting that might be, it was important for her to show Drakyn that she could take command of this situation and resolve it. She needed even more to demonstrate to Krell and his minions that she was a formidable enemy, and not simply a victim in this situation or any other. They would face retribution for their actions. She quickly sensed and then heard Drakyn's movements, and knew that he was headed toward her in his single-minded intent to protect her.

Honor was now moving soundlessly through the catwalk platforms, once again above the big equipment assembly hall, when she saw two familiar catlike forms down below. One big felinoid was being half-dragged between two of the Wolfen officers. The other moved stiff-legged and angry, but unhurt. Merlin was clearly furious, with the thick tuft of dark gray fur at the back of his neck spiked high. Tarquin's shaggy dark fur was streaked and matted with fresh blood that left a trail upon the deck as he struggled to keep pace with his captors. Both felinoids were heavily shackled with metal mitts covering their paws, rendering their claws useless.

***

KRELL was in an extremely foul temper. He had been summoned urgently to Engineering where an unexplained power drain was impeding all attempts to increase speed. The engineers and technicians were unable to determine any reason for the problem, as

Honor: Drakyn's Lady

a diagnostic check showed the equipment running at 95% efficiency. Yet, when the drive was engaged it invariably lost power again. At this rate Krell suspected they might never reach Wolfen home space. Krell's senses warned him not to ignore inexplicable occurrences, especially knowing that the female was still running free somewhere aboard the ship. It was imperative that he regain control again!

When an officer named Kando had reported the capture of the two felinoids, Krell had ordered them brought to him in shackles. He was delighted to have prisoners, and he was certain that they could be used against that damned pirate female who so plagued his mind. The older felinoid limped badly and trailed blood as he was half-dragged into the chamber. The younger one glared at Krell in a manner than reminded him of the woman, and that made the Wolfen captain smile. Felinoids generally died loudly and well, given the opportunity to do so.

Krell listened to Kando's quick report on how the two were captured, and how their distant ship was spotted. The captain was controlling himself against the urge to strike out at the officer's gloating tone of voice.

Instead of commenting, Krell went to a comlink on the wall and contacted his bridge, growling, "Vens, the two intruders aboard have been captured. Scan for their ship and destroy it immediately! Blow up a few of those asteroids, too, if necessary!"

He then turned away from the link and was about to speak to the prisoners when the emergency klaxon began its shrill warning sound, and the lighting cut back to half power. Krell immediately pulled out his blaster.

A technician hurried forward from the area of the anti-matter reactors, shouting in alarm, "My lord Krell! The star drive engines are now on a massive power build up! Safety controls are totally disabled, and the master override has been somehow countermanded and frozen!"

"Sabotage!" Kando spat, jerking out his blade and thrusting it at the already-wounded felinoid.

Krell snarled and used his own weapon to knock the blade from its target, sending it skittering across the deck and under some equipment.

Just in that same moment there was a loud cry from above

their heads and one of the Wolfen security guards who patrolled above fell from the maze of overhead catwalks. The body hit the deck with a final-sounding crunch, as his uniform tore open and his bloody throat was revealed.

Scrambling out of the way of the body, Krell propelled both prisoners away from himself as he moved. Tarquin fell to all fours on the deck. Merlin managed to stay on his two feet, but Krell easily yanked him over to use as a personal shield. Red energy beams snaked downward from the catwalks and two of them disappeared in bursts of fiery energy as others scattered.

There was a long moment of silent inaction as Krell, Kando, and two other officers squinted upward into the dimness, searching for their attacker in the labyrinth of platforms and catwalks above them.

Now Krell pressed his own blaster up under Merlin's chin as the Wolfen called out, "Show yourself, Honor! Your human sentimentality is so predictable! Prove how you value this feline's life!"

When there was no immediate response, Krell met Kando's eyes and nodded toward the obviously wounded felinoid at their feet. Kando quickly grasped Tarquin by his disabled paws and dragged him out of sight, around a corner of the corridor, leaving a trail of blood behind them.

"Tarquin!" Merlin exclaimed in concern but halted when Krell jammed the blaster even harder into his throat.

"I will burn off this cat's head, Honor!" Krell announced loudly. "Then we'll drain the blood from the other one and find a painful way to kill him, too. Their ship has already been located and destroyed. They cannot escape us!"

"You are wasting the little bit of time I've left you, Krell," Honor's voice rang out overhead. "You know that the power build-up is my doing." She dropped gracefully from the catwalk, landing upon her feet before the Wolfen commander. She held a blaster rifle leveled at Krell, and now stood at point-blank range.

Smoothly, Krell asked, "So, you've decided to kill us all, bitch? Perhaps you seek to impress me with your courage?"

Her gaze measured him, and he had the distinct impression that she was disdainful of what she saw. "Your people can't stop the power build up. Only I can. Your engineers can run over every possible line before time runs out, and it will soon. They won't find the answer much less make the necessary corrections in time. I estimate that you have less than 15 standard time ticks left."

"Your price?" Krell hissed between clenched teeth.

"Set the felinoids free. They meant well coming after me, but I prefer to keep this battle between you and me! Put them into my two-man shuttle—and it is the only shuttle I've left space-worthy by the way—and release them unmolested. In return for their freedom, I'll remain on board with you and stop the build-up. I'll also release your star drive. I think you've already noticed that it wasn't working quite right."

"The little pirate shows nobility?" Krell sneered.

Her laugh was dry. "Hardly, Krell. My intent is merely to clear the field for us. You and me. The true battle, the real struggle has first and always been between us, my dear old *friend*. For reasons none of these others even suspect. If possible, I would send away all of your foolish crew so we could be alone to finish this the way it began, when you RAN away from me!"

Krell snarled an oath at Honor, but she merely laughed again, and added, "You'd better warn Kando not to come into range, or I'll burn a big hole in him."

Ignoring the warning, Krell pondered aloud, "Perhaps I shall allow this ship to destroy itself, as we all move forward to death in any case."

"Death by inaction is for cowards who cry when they bleed," Honor quoted a Wolfen proverb and then grinned at him insolently. "Unlike you, I do not face immediate danger. How many times have you tried to kill me or have me killed, believed you had succeeded, and then found you had utterly failed? You've always failed. Failed! This ship may destroy itself and everyone else on board, but I will survive. You will always fail to kill me. I promise you that."

Merlin blinked at Honor, knowing a huge bluff when he heard it. He knew very well how powerful Honor and Drakyn both were—and what their vulnerabilities were. As a child she had taught him a human card game: poker. She was playing for very high stakes just now, and the fact that she did not meet his eyes told him that Honor did not want any distraction from him. He kept silent, despite his concerns.

Honor continued speaking to Krell, saying, "I am offering you a chance to get what you've always claimed you want, Krell. Let Merlin and Tarquin go, and I will stay aboard with you." She paused and then added, "You'd best hurry, aging one!"

"No, Honor!" Merlin said involuntarily, "You can't do this!"

"Hush, Merlin," she chided him gently. "It's my option here." Then to Krell, she said, "Hurry, Krell. The ship requires your decision."

Krell drew himself to his full height and stepped toward her. She did not move.

With rough intensity, the Wolfen said, "You know what I require from you—your secrets, your power, your blood! I want what keeps you young and strong!"

"My life secrets?" she remarked wryly, and then nodded as if fully expecting his reply. With a squaring of her shoulders, she said, "Agreed, then. The felinoids leave in the shuttle first, unmolested. Everything you wish to discover, I will show you— but only YOU, Krell. Decide. Now!" The alarms began to sound again, louder and more urgently.

Kando called out, "My commander, there are less than 10 *tups* before the process is irreversible!"

Krell leaned over Honor and hissed, "I shall require even more of you, woman! True, I want your blood secrets, but also more! You will not only remain aboard this ship, you will surrender yourself to me! You will remain by my side, bound to me as your lord. Do you swear this?"

"No!" Merlin protested again.

Honor seemed not to hear him as she smiled tightly at Krell, almost appearing amused as she replied, "I swear it by the blood in my veins. By my *human* life." Then her smile turned dangerous. "I also swear that I will make you miserable as long as you live!"

"You intrigue me!" Krell exulted, turning to face Kando who was now holding a blaster on Merlin's head. "Take the felinoids to the small shuttle the woman arrived in. Make certain of its SAFE ejection from this ship."

Kando gasped his assent, somewhat awestruck by the agreement he had just witnessed between the human female and his commander.

Honor: Drakyn's Lady

Wrapped in darkness and silence on the catwalk above them, Drakyn observed the confrontation between Honor and Krell, and listened in admiration at Honor's skill as she maneuvered the Wolfen commander toward her intended terms. Beneath the calmly mocking façade that Honor presented to Krell, her smoldering anger was growing. When Tarquin's wounded body was dragged away from the area, Drakyn silently followed from above. The Wolfen officer dropped the felinoid in a cubicle and returned to the confrontation. Drakyn slipped down from his vantage point, a moving shadow amid the confusion Honor had so successfully generated on this ship. The rising pitch of the repeating alarms indicated that time was growing short, but it scarcely concerned Drakyn. The smell of Tarquin's blood drew him irresistibly to investigate his wounds. The felinoid lay on his side in the middle of the cubicle deck, his red blood a puddle beneath his deep wound. Drakyn could scarcely hear Tarquin's breathing now, and the few shallow breaths in evidence seemed to be a bubbling effort.

Without hesitation, Drakyn reached down and touched Tarquin's head, his powerful brain reaching to the one in distress.

Chapter 17

Sabotage

HONOR insisted upon personally witnessing the safe release of her felinoid friends. She kept a cautious distance between herself and Krell, despite the fact that she knew the Wolfen ship's time was running out.

Krell gestured toward a cubicle where Tarquin's big gray form lay on his side, a puddle of blood near his wound. "Pick up your companion, cat. Carry him to that shuttle, unless you wish to leave him behind."

Merlin leaned over Tarquin to do just that, but was startled when his father figure rolled over and met his gaze alertly. "I will walk like a warrior. I will not be carried like a mewling kitten!"

"Move quickly now," Honor urged seriously, yet seeming unruffled.

Catching hold of her shoulder, Merlin said urgently, "Honor, we can fight them…"

Honor put a finger to his mouth, stopping him. "We will, but not now. There's no time, and this ship's going to blow up if I don't act soon. There are times when promises, even those made to a sworn enemy, take precedence over other desires. Trust me!"

Merlin resisted going to the *Freedom* ship, looking to Honor and calling out: "I won't abandon you, Honor!"

Frowning just slightly, she met his gaze and replied, "Your

safety is more important than mine just now, kitty-cat. Go and pursue your own destiny, as I am following my own. Others need you, Merlin of Viste, and you, Tarquin of Viste. Go in peace now, and quickly!" Then she embraced Merlin strongly for a moment, pressing her face against his. He was startled to hear her voice inside his head: "Get my ship out of here. I know Gall is out there waiting for your orders. Rendezvous with the *Serpentine* and then, if necessary, chase this ship back into the Wolfen empire. The Wolfen MUST *not* keep my shuttle! It is imperative, Merlin! Be relentless!"

From across the chamber, Krell hissed, "Bid your friends a fond farewell, Honor. You will not see them again!" His eyes fixed on Tarquin for a moment, appearing a bit puzzled.

Honor released Merlin immediately before Krell tried to drag her away, and Honor's hard expression gave Merlin the final nudge he required. He knew that he really had actually heard her thoughts, and no matter what occurred on this ship now, Honor was not really alone. Drakyn's presence was still unknown to the Wolfen. If Honor was so concerned about getting her ship away from the Wolfen, it must hold something extremely important. He would obey Honor. Plus, his own oath to the Fleet required that he treat the Wolfen ship as the enemy it was.

From the network of catwalks above, Drakyn was able to soundlessly follow and observe as Honor insisted upon supervising the safe and immediate release of the two felinoids. It occurred to Drakyn that if the young one had listened to his orders to remain aboard the *Nobleseed*, their injuries and this necessity could have been avoided, but they may have been killed by now if the Wolfen destroyed his ship. He knew the young Fleet captain well enough not to be surprised by his headstrong and rather reckless independent action, and was a bit proud of him.

It pleased Drakyn to hear Honor seriously direct Merlin and Tarquin to flee far away from the vicinity of this Wolfen ship. He was easily able to understand her unspoken request for Merlin to remove himself from involvement in this situation. She was very aware of his Fleet responsibilities and how the Wolfen would be delighted to keep Merlin captive as well if they were aware that he was a Fleet officer. Honor clearly had no intention of remaining Krell's captive very much longer; she would most certainly allow this ship to destroy itself before returning to the Wolfen home world with him. Honor was the injured and abused party in this situation and she had already indicated to him that she wanted to handle this Wolfen Captain Krell in her own way. So Drakyn decided he would watch Honor, and take his cues from her actions. No matter what else occurred, Drakyn had no intention of allowing Krell to survive this encounter.

Not seeing any alternatives, Merlin swung himself up into Honor's little shuttle ship after Tarquin. Still hampered by the metallic mittens, he hit the hatch control to seal and pressurize the ship. More than anything he wanted to stop this, but he had to trust Honor, despite all his misgivings.

Turning now to Tarquin, Merlin watched him as he used his huge teeth to tear away the metallic mitts that covered his paws, dropping them to the deck. "Where is the main power toggle on this ship?" the elder felinoid growled.

Merlin was busily tearing the mitts from his own paws, and in moments he also was able to discard them. He then slipped into the seat beside Tarquin and together they activated the ship's systems while observing the space doors opening before them.

"Can we get a weapons' status?" Merlin muttered, punching buttons and frowning. "Honor keeps this ship armed!"

"The Wolfen fused the weapons power feed lines," Tarquin stated calmly, his own paw tips moving efficiently over the controls, "and if we tried to fire, the backlash would destroy us. Also, if we tried to dock with the *Nobleseed*, the docking apparatus would be tripped and blow us both out of space. We must get clear. Contact the *Serpentine* and have Gall come and meet us. Then we can go after the Wolfen with a ship properly prepared to fight them!" He glanced at Merlin. "Drakyn came to me. He stopped my bleeding and gave me specific orders…"

Neither of them spoke for a short time as the shuttle slipped free of the Wolfen ship, out into space. They used short energy pulses to move out the proper distance from the bigger ship before they began to fully activate the shuttle's star drive engines.

Merlin said, "Honor wants this ship well away from the Wolfen. She also told me to contact Gall. She would not be quite so concerned about her shuttle unless it holds information she's concerned about falling into Wolfen hands."

"Quite likely," Tarquin agreed with a hiss.

***

KRELL stood over Honor like a guard as she worked on the Wolfen ship's engines. Three technicians also stood nearby, watching every move she made—as if they could stop her before she did something fatal to the ship.

Smiling to herself, Honor wondered briefly where Drakyn was at the moment. Internally, the woman quickly projected a very precise request to Drakyn, who heard her immediately and was more than pleased to agree. It took her less than two standard ticks to adjust the equipment, and the power indicators receded at once. The alarms stopped their bleating call, leaving an abrupt silence. Honor regarded her adjustments for a moment or two longer before she straightened up and looked at the nearest technician as if expecting his approval.

On cue, the Wolfen reported, "Power levels are stabilizing and dropping, commander Krell. They are already down to acceptable ranges." His gaze was a mixture of awe and resentment as he regarded Honor. She smiled powerfully at him, causing the Wolfen to twitch involuntarily.

Now Krell's rough hand caught the back of her neck, turning her to face him. She did not resist as he dragged her away from the Engineering section. Snapping commands in Wolfen language to his subordinates, he inquired about power levels and the position of Honor's shuttle. He glowered when he heard that the *Revenge*'s weapons' power had been drained to minimal by the reactor build-up and further depleted when they had fired upon the felinoid's ship. The weapons were only beginning to recharge. His frown became deeper still when it was reported that the shuttle had leapt away at five-plus—a rate none of them had imagined the tiny craft was capable of producing.

Snarling to himself, Krell pulled Honor into a lift, shut the doors, and turned on her. "You are mine now, Honor. Your friends were eager to desert you!"

Not showing her own thoughts about that, Honor merely replied, "As I pointed out, this is our battle, not theirs."

He suddenly pulled her against him, the armored spikes on his belt and boots jabbing at her body. Deliberately, he twisted her weaker arm behind her back. Honor did not struggle, nor did she cooperate with his mocking caresses. When she finally uttered an involuntary murmur of pain, Krell released her, his eyes bright with triumph.

Coldly, Honor stared at him. "Krell, I am bound by my promise to stay with you on this ship. But only that. If you still want to learn how I became powerful, the first step will be for me to drink some of YOUR blood—without killing you. It would be very easy and appealing to me to lose my temper during that first step, and simply eliminate you. Even with a guard standing there, you'll have no choice but to trust me in that first moment. Are your egotistic glandular needs going to outweigh your desire for youth and strength?"

"Give me your secrets! Now!" he demanded harshly.

Honor thumbed the lift control to halt the car where it was. She turned her face toward his and said, "Very well. I'll keep my promises, Krell. I must taste your blood first!"

Drawing out a knife, Krell grasped the front of Honor's metallic cloth bodysuit with one hand and easily lifted her from the floor, holding her so that her face was level with his own. The sharp blade dented the material of her suit just below her left breast; the slightest bit more pressure would drive the knife into her heart.

"Yes." Krell's smile was wide and ugly. "Now! While I hold you thus!"

Unable to recoil from his Wolfen scent, Honor said softly, "As you wish. You'll feel the bite, but a brave warrior like yourself should be able to handle it."

Resting a hand on his shoulder, Honor drew in a breath and then effortlessly ripped open the collar of his uniform, smiling in a manner that showed her sharpened blood teeth to him. She whispered: "My bite will introduce enzymes into your bloodstream that will immediately make you almost immune to any illness. A few swallows will suffice."

She lowered her mouth to his now-exposed throat, filling her mind with images of things Krell had done to her. Her teeth easily cut through his tough skin. His low grunt of pain made it possible for her to allow the bitter and unappetizing blood to fill her mouth and then slide down her throat without enjoyment or satisfaction. She purposely kept her mind cold and angry, concentrating upon the task she performed until her stomach rebelled involuntarily. She gagged, stopped drinking, and pulled back from him.

Krell dropped her and staggered back. His suddenly numb fingers released the knife and it fell near their feet.

Honor had slipped down to her knees, wrapping her arms around her stomach. She fought waves of nausea; her eyes watered, and she concentrated on breathing steadily to soothe herself. When the sick feeling passed, she noticed that her own blood stained one sleeve; Krell's knife had nicked her skin slightly.

Krell blinked at her in obvious confusion for a moment and then visibly collected himself. Lowering his brows in irritation, he growled, "It pleases me to see you on your knees before me. You will find yourself there often in the future. What else must be done to complete the process?"

Honor raised her head, smiling at him in her insolent manner, and replied, "Half a day from now I will drink your blood again. THEN you will drink mine, and you will experience something quite different from the last time!"

The Wolfen captain grasped her arm, pulled her close against him, and snarled, "Why wait? I can do that now!"

Calmly, she returned, "Sure you can, but you'll go mad again. Your body needs time to assimilate the enzymes my saliva has introduced into your veins. A little patience, please!"

"If you are lying to me, I will see you gutted and I will eat your beating heart!" Krell glared at her a moment longer before pushing her slightly back and reaching for the lift controls. A moment later the lift continued its path to the bridge.

***

AFTER Krell took Honor away from Engineering, the technicians quickly dispersed to their individual posts. When all but one technician had left the area, Drakyn silently dropped down from his observation point above. The Wolfen tech scarcely had time to gasp before Drakyn's strong hand silenced him. Then Drakyn opened the control board hatch himself and entered a one-word command Honor had communicated to him. For a moment an alarm light flashed, but then it stopped. No klaxon sounded; no clock showed that the original self-destruct instructions had been re-initiated on a new countdown. The Wolfen ship was now doomed.

Honor: Drakyn's Lady

Smiling proudly at Honor's talents, Drakyn closed the control hatch again and then proceeded to follow in the direction his lady had gone. He doubted that she really needed his assistance now, and it seemed justified that she should personally take action against Krell, but Drakyn saw nothing wrong with clearing the field of other adversaries.

***

THERE was still a scent of blood and death and decay on the bridge, though the deck was wet as if it had recently been scrubbed down. Honor fought the urge to gag again at the odors, and found that breathing through her mouth seemed to help. Only two senior officers now occupied the bridge area — one in the command seat and the other at the navigation and weapons boards. At the appearance of Krell and Honor, the one at command immediately rose and moved to a lesser post. Krell assumed the command position and gestured for Honor to stand at his left hand, traditionally where a Wolfen servitor stood.

Honor observed the two officers eye her and then exchange silently meaningful glances, but she maintained her upbeat, amused expression. She knew it was irritating Krell. Actually she really was pleased to stand close to Krell's side. From there she was easily able to observe the changing navigational readouts at helm control. The instructions she had embedded into the ship's main computer to commandeer helm control and re-initiate the countdown would activate the moment Drakyn input the password she had communicated to him, but the effects would be initiated in gradual stages, giving her a bit more time before it was noticed.

Suddenly the lift doors opened and Bersunn stumbled onto the bridge, his tunic torn and stained with dark blood. He bumped into the officer at the navigation post, snarled at Honor and then backed away, chuckling to himself as he remarked, "Captain, there is a human on your bridge!"

Honor watched Krell as the Wolfen captain glared at Bersunn impatiently, yet he hesitated for a heartbeat before declaring, "You're still out of control, Bersunn. Go away until you sleep it off!" Then he turned back toward his monitor readouts.

"Out of control?" Bersunn echoed in a wavering tone, "Who has control over any of this? HE's here, and cannot be resisted.

He'll snare us all with his burning eyes and long teeth, and then he will reel us in until there's no hope, no help, nothing but the burning and the drinking and the dying!" As if to demonstrate, the medical officer raised his forearm and bit deeply into his flesh, growling again as he greedily sucked at the blood.

Krell and the two other officers were momentarily silent, shocked at this latest demonstration of what they took to be the madness caused by blood drinking.

"Call Security," Krell commanded quietly. He looked hard at Honor for a moment and then locked his gaze upon the obviously mad creature who was now crooning slightly as he continued to savage his own arm.

Honor was certain that Drakyn had caused this new manifestation of madness, but she merely remarked in a clear voice, "It's the next stage of blood insanity. I've never seen it this bad before. He's been drinking the spoiled blood of those already dead!"

"Silence!" Krell snarled at her, not taking his eyes away from Bersunn.

The mad one now released his bite, then leaned his head back and spat blood upward, causing the gore to spray over everyone and crying out, "I can't drink it! It's tainted by him! His blood is poison, and it will destroy all of us, maybe even him! You cursed us, Krell! You should have resisted this bitch!"

All three of the Wolfen officers were staring at the doctor now, their attention nervously diverted from their posts.

Glaring at Honor with sunken eyes, Bersunn shouted, "YOU brought this infection among us! You are responsible! I burn!" He grabbed at her but then drew back abruptly as if he expected to be hurt by the touch. "Where is he—the one with the burning eyes? Krell, he hides from us!"

"Restrain him!" Krell ordered sharply. "Where is Security?"

"You probably ate them," Honor suggested, grinning wickedly.

Immediately one of the officers grasped Bersunn's arm but was nearly thrown off, and the other officer leapt to assist him.

Only Honor saw the helm control adjust itself, just as her embedded programming had instructed it; the ship's speed was now increasing considerably. After two heartbeats, the readings reverted to where they had been prior to the increase, but

Honor's finely-honed senses could feel the difference in the ship. Their speed would continue to climb, slowly and steadily, and the readings would continue to hide this fact for a short but precious period.

Everyone, including Honor, was a bit startled when the lift doors slid open again and two Security troopers entered the bridge with weapons drawn. Honor smiled at what she could hear coming from Drakyn's mind to hers.

Krell opened his mouth to give an order, but Bersunn let out a screeching roar, broke free, and threw himself upon the nearest trooper, clawing at the neck of the man's uniform, ripping flesh and clothing as he went for his throat. For several heartbeats the bridge was in chaos as the five Wolfen struggled to regain control of the Wolfen physician. Finally they managed to pin him to the deck and secure him with magnetic cuffs. Even restrained, Bersunn continued to howl and snap at them, completely out of his mind.

Seeing that the mad one was now helpless, Krell stepped back, ordering, "Lock him up somewhere! Now!"

The two Security personnel hauled Bersunn to his feet and dragged him into the lift. The doors quickly snapped shut behind them, leaving the three Wolfen officers alone on the bridge, one of them holding his left arm. He had been bitten during the fray, but he moved toward his weapons post without remark.

"Give me a report of the ship's status!" Krell ordered quietly, still breathing a bit hard from the effort. Then he shouted, "Honor, you are to stand here, at my side!"

It required only another heartbeat to realize that Honor was no longer on the bridge.

Chapter 18

Destruction

DURING the melee among the Wolfen, Honor had ducked past the flailing claws and jaws and had stepped into a tiny sanitary cubicle just behind Krell's command post. She did not even manage to close the half-door when a strong hand reached down from above and caught her left upper arm. She was easily and silently hauled upward into the maze of conduits, wiring, and environmental ducts above.

"Little one," Drakyn breathed close to her ear, his lips touching her cheek for only a moment while his foot pushed the ceiling tile back into its place with enough force to jam it tightly.

Smiling, she nuzzled against him for a moment. "Hello, you. Time is short. Let's get out of here, sweetie!"

Silently now, they moved together away from the bridge area and toward the shuttle bays. Moving closely beside Honor, Drakyn's mind heard what hers told him, and he was very aware of how confident Honor was feeling at the moment, yet he still had reservations about their escape from this ship. Honor's nature refused to surrender to the angry urge to kill her enemies using her physical strength, but in his opinion she was rather too confident about her alternate plan's success. Just because things were proceeding as she wished at the moment, something unexpected could still happen. Drakyn would have been much more comfortable had Honor simply stepped back and allowed him to execute all of these Wolfen animals.

He resisted this urge, knowing it was her battle more than his, and he wanted to keep peace with her. He focused upon her lovely profile and allowed himself to smile just a bit, considering how unimaginably dreary his life would still be if she had never come to Viste. He knew that the time of their exclusive relationship was coming to an end, yet he refused to allow himself to surrender to the inevitable. "Anything and everything" was what she had promised, and given him, upon their first meeting, and he would willingly and forever give the same to her.

His attention was drawn back to the events at hand when Honor gestured for him to halt and then pointed to the corridor below. They would need to go down to enter the pressurized shuttle bay area. However, an armed Wolfen trooper stood guarding the sealed portal.

"I'll distract him," she whispered. Then she slithered back around a curve in the corridor where she dropped down without waiting for his agreement.

Drakyn watched as Honor came around the corner at ramming speed, but then stopped in her tracks in apparent surprise, with hands raised slightly in a gesture of surrender to the guard. Her gaze centered intensely upon the Wolfen before her.

The Wolfen officer touched a comlink on the portal frame, clearly intending to contact his captain. During the instant that his eyes were directed away from the woman, Drakyn slid down from his position above and landed almost soundlessly between the Wolfen and the portal.

Drakyn looked at Honor as he grasped the Wolfen's wrist and crushed it effortlessly, while his other strong arm wrapped around the creature's neck to stop him from crying out. A moment later the officer's unconscious form fell in a limp heap to the deck at Drakyn's feet.

"Are you ready to go now, little one?" Drakyn asked her, pressing the door access panel with a thumb. The portal slid open without hesitation.

Honor grinned as she threw herself forward into his arms with enough energy to make Drakyn stagger back into the shuttle bay. Pressing her face happily into his chest for a moment, Honor stated, "Anywhere, anytime, sweetie!"

Just then the ship lurched violently and alarms began to wail suddenly around them.

Honor merely raised her head and looked up at Drakyn, remarking dryly, "Sounds like this ship's in trouble. The systems will be overloading already. What a shame! At least Merlin and Tarquin are safe and clear of this ship. You and I can handle anything Krell tries to do to us!" She grinned up at him.

Drakyn smiled back at her and put a gentle hand to the side of her delicate face. "You always amaze me, Honor. You have endured a kind of personal hell aboard this ship, and yet you continue to worry about others, take action to help them escape first, and now pause to chuckle about tricks played upon your greatest enemy! Have I ever thanked you for coming to Viste, coming to my universe, and making me feel alive again after many, many empty years?"

"Not in words, love, but always in your actions," Honor answered sincerely. She reached up to put her arms around his neck, bringing his face down closer to hers so that she might kiss him. Her lips brushed his first, and then the kiss deepened and grew into an all-encompassing expression of the hunger they both felt for each other.

Drakyn lifted her from her feet and held her close against his broad chest. Raising his face at last, he whispered, "This is unwise just now. This ship is self-destructing, and the Wolfen are undoubtedly coming here."

"So, who said we were wise?" she returned, kissing him again and again, wanting to literally lose herself in the sensory experience of touching him and of loving him. "Living on the edge, are we?"

"Honor..!" Drakyn kissed her again, thoroughly, before whispering, "Their numbers decline. The ship is doomed. That lunatic medic will kill until he is killed. We need not remain aboard."

Honor recognized the pleased expression on Drakyn's face. It meant he was enjoying himself too, which was usually a sign of great danger. She knew how violent he could become. They both had been given more than minimum provocation recently, but she was better at resisting the urge to violence than he was. She knew better than to encourage him to tarry here.

Shaking her head to clear it of distractions, Honor told him, "You should go. I'm not ready yet."

"Honor!" he rumbled, reaching for her.

"No," she disagreed quietly but firmly. "I've come this far with this much effort, I won't walk away from Krell without being certain of his end."

Frowning now, the big man shook his head unhappily. "I dislike this, Honor. The risk is…"

"…is mine to take," she interrupted quickly, smiling. "You've made me strong and independent. Let me use these abilities."

Drakyn mused aloud, "I could stop you."

"Perhaps," she agreed with a challenging grin. "But perhaps not!"

Drakyn's hand touched Honor under her chin, tilting her face upward toward his own. The dark eyes that had captivated her from their first encounter sparkled down at her, revealing a depth of emotion he could never voice. Honor reached up and lightly touched the man's cheek, letting her own expression answer his before their lips met again. For another moment she allowed herself to lean against his chest, safe and content in his sheltering arms.

"Come back to Viste," he said, as a request, not a demand. "Come back to me."

"Soon," she promised him.

Suddenly Honor felt herself thrown backward onto the deck with Drakyn's heavy weight holding her down. An unexpected burning pain lanced through her at the level of her collarbone.

Drakyn pulled himself up from her and she stared at the length of sharpened metal rod that protruded from his chest. This had also wounded her. Drakyn's face contorted in agony as he reached behind himself and grasped the rod to pull it out. Slipping to her knees, Honor reached up and helped Drakyn pull the two-meter long rod out of his back, flinching herself at his involuntary grunt of pain as they did so. She then saw who their attackers were: three security officers.

One of them reached for Honor and Drakyn caught him in an easy, one-handed grip that audibly broke the Wolfen's neck. A second guard rushed at them and Drakyn launched the first guard's body at him before snatching up the bloody rod. He threw it with deadly accuracy and effectively fastened the Wolfen to a wall like a mounted insect. The third guard came at Honor as she got to her feet. Honor caught and threw him down as well, crushing his windpipe. She then turned to tend to Drakyn's wound, subliminally aware that her own hand and arm were stiff with pain.

Krell was suddenly there. He knocked her aside and rushed past her, holding yet another of those sharpened metal rods.

Certain that Honor could handle the guard she had tackled, Drakyn paused to regard the painful and bloody wound that had pierced him through from rear shoulder to breast. He was internally commanding his flesh to close and heal itself when the metal rod Krell brandished struck him mid-chest like a lance. The momentum knocked him backward, the razor-sharp end of the rod sliced easily and deeply into his chest cavity, piercing through into his heart muscle.

The sound Drakyn uttered was more one of surprise than distress.

Unaware that she was herself screaming, Honor physically attacked Krell. Her slim arm went around his rough throat, cutting off his air. She exerted her considerable strength and sheer force to dislodge him from Drakyn. They struggled as she tried to get a grip on the rod, now slippery with Drakyn's darkly spurting blood. She finally was able to shove Krell backward with enough force to knock him against the side of a shuttle with an echoing boom. Gasping for breath, she then managed to yank the rod free from Drakyn's flesh and threw it, clattering to the ground.

As Honor did so, her gaze met Drakyn's. She could feel his agonized helplessness dismay, and increasing disorientation. She reached down to cover the gaping wound in his chest with her hand, as if to somehow lend her strength to his, to help him try and heal himself. Drakyn's big hand grasped her free one in a familiar possessive gesture, his flesh suddenly so cold that it seemed to burn hers.

Then, in a heartbeat, his body was suddenly gone, seeming to melt away like fog in strong sunlight.

Honor could not move. The memory of his burning, feverish eyes held her immobile.

Drakyn was gone, not even leaving dust behind.

Honor knelt there with her hand extended downward,

blinking in disbelief. She had no idea what this meant. Never before had she even seen Drakyn actually wounded. Her mind recoiled from the very idea of his life endangered, his physical body inexplicably dissolved! This bewildered, alarmed, and then infuriated her. She turned slowly toward Krell who was painfully struggling to his feet, smirking in his triumph. He was startled and overbalanced when she launched herself at him, and he fell heavily onto the deck. The fury in her face filled him with numbing alarm; it was unlike any expression he had ever seen on her.

Effortlessly, she ripped back Krell's heavy tunic with her fingernails and easily shoved his arms away as she fastened her teeth onto the large vein in his neck. It was not at all difficult for her to hold down his shoulders while she drank deeply of his blood. This unimaginable anger and the taste of his growing terror made her enemy's blood palatable this time. She wanted to kill him this way. She wanted to absorb away his full life force and leave him a shriveled hunk of meat. She wanted, she needed, revenge!

However, at that moment a sound, a voice—familiar and yet not so—echoed within her consciousness and stopped her cold.

Releasing the Wolfen commander, Honor leapt to her feet and stared around the empty corridors, a name unspoken upon her blood-wet lips. *Did she hear his voice? Did she?* The metal rod rested nearby, with the blood still heavy upon it.

She pushed her hair out of her eyes with a stiff hand, and drew a deep, calming breath.

Coldly under control again, Honor looked down at Krell. Enough of his blood had been taken to make him slow and lethargic. His eyes were anxiously fixed upon her, a new sort of fear evident in them. Somehow seeing his terror satisfied her. She drew another deep breath for control and then picked up the rod, weighing it thoughtfully in her hand as she told Krell conversationally, "What I really ought to do is pin you to that deck like the bug you are!"

Krell moved his arms, unsuccessfully trying to pull himself up.

Softly and calmly, Honor told the Wolfen, "Unlike you, I am not a murderer. You have caused the deaths of so many! All along you have been driven by fear and jealousy. Fear of me and the cowardice I bring out in you. Even more, fear of your own aging body and approaching death. Any of your original crew would have gone laughing to his death in an honorable battle, as a Wolfen warrior. You've denied them that. You are going to die, Krell, but not at my hands, without any reprieve from me or what I could do to you. Your death will be caused by your own foolish errors. I will know when death claims you, and I will celebrate the victory!"

Humiliation burned on Krell's face. His brain searched for a way to save the situation, to turn it back to his own favor. All he could finally say was, "You gave me your word!" Shakily, he pulled himself to his knees.

Leaning over him like a mother admonishing a difficult child, Honor whispered, "I bluffed, and you fell for it. Sue me." She straightened up again, blinking to eliminate the white spots floating before her eyes.

Baring his own teeth, Krell threw himself recklessly at her.

The impact of his weight knocked her against a wall and for a moment the world went red with pain. Even through this she was easily able to shove Krell's hands away from her and she picked up and swung the rod at him. It struck the side of his head, knocking him down, dazed. For a heartbeat Honor seriously again considered finishing him, but then she threw the rod away far down the deck, sneering, "You aren't even worth the vengeance."

Turning, Honor walked away from Krell. Deliberately, she punched at a pressure valve as she passed it, releasing a vast cloud of white propulsion gases into the area. It effectively hid her path from his gaze.

Honor knew he would not dare to follow her. She then hurried to an Engineering terminal to check the settings she had encoded into the ship's systems. She wanted to be certain that all was as she wished it to be. It occurred to her that it was growing more difficult to see, as some of the gases that she had released were making their way along the deck and into the Engineering area. The gases cleared as she moved away from the source back toward the shuttle bay, but a strangely gathering whiteness in her brain still obscured her vision. The pain from her shoulder had intensified and she felt the warmth of new blood running down her right arm and dripping from her hand.

The shuttle bay was deserted. Despite what she had told Krell about disabling all of the shuttles, she knew she could still use one of them to depart this doomed ship. Honor staggered a bit as she found the spot where she had hidden an environmental suit. Just remaining on her feet seemed to require an enormous effort. She was struggling into the suit when the increasing whiteness unexpectedly turned black. Honor felt herself slip down to the deck, losing consciousness.

***

THE *Serpentine* had quickly spotted the *Freedom* shuttle and came to meet the escaping ship. As Merlin had promised Honor, he sent an urgent message to Gall and soon they were able to safely berth Honor's shuttle aboard the larger ship and well beyond the *Revenge's* weapons range. The *Serpentine* kept its distance monitoring space where the Wolfen ship was located, trusting that Honor and Drakyn would soon escape as well. It was not long before Merlin and Tarquin were on the bridge of the big ship with Gall, carefully watching the sensor consoles that showed the very distant position of the Wolfen ship.

"No sign of escape pods," Tarquin growled softly, "The ship's speed is increasing steadily, but it has not measurably changed its course."

Sighing tightly, Merlin fought the urge to change the *Serpentine's* own course to intercept the distant ship. Opening fire upon the Wolfen could interfere with whatever Honor was doing. Surely she had a plan, but what was it? Drakyn would never allow something to happen to Honor.

Merlin said aloud: "I know Honor's going to do something!"

"This isn't good," Gall pronounced, from the engineering monitors. "I now see very unstable readings from that ship. Her outer hull appears to be heating very rapidly. Major structural damage should commence within the next 20 ticks."

"Come on, Honor!" Merlin whispered like a prayer. He looked at the communications boards and saw the *Revenge's* signals collapse and disappear just as the monitor screens flashed white.

Hissing loudly, Tarquin snarled, "A massive explosion! The ship's broken into a thousand pieces. They're dead! Secure for the shock wave!"

The resulting shockwave from the *Revenge's* explosion reverberated in the silence of space, moving outward like ripples in a still pond, disturbing small pieces of dust and stray asteroids alike. Pieces of the destroyed ship created a massive debris field, much of which either burned up as they entered the atmosphere of a nearby planetoid, or else stabilized into a slow orbit around that body. The process continued until the reaction literally exhausted its energy, and chunks of melted metal and other materials continued to be propelled in all directions.

Merlin watched what occurred, keeping his jaw locked in silence, unwilling and unable to voice his very real fears for the fates of both Drakyn and Honor. Without asking for concurrence from the others, Merlin gave the order to guide the *Serpentine* into the debris field, scanning each larger piece for the possibility that it might be an escape pod, and then moving on. Slowly they continued the search.

It was difficult to resist the nagging sense of unease Merlin felt with regard to Honor and Lord Drakyn. Merlin struggled silently against the strength of his own emotions as he piloted the *Serpentine* through the debris field that was the remains of the Wolfen ship, scanning each and every piece of debris for signs of life, of survivors. The power of whatever had caused the blast had reduced the ship itself to pieces, many no larger than a standard meter. The chances of survivors grew dimmer as time ticked by. Nevertheless, with the calm and patience of a feline hunting, Merlin meticulously continued his scans.

He wondered silently if Honor had simply allowed the self-destruct to take the Wolfen ship. It seemed unlikely, because the Wolfen captain would undoubtedly have insisted upon Honor keeping her word to stop the process immediately after Merlin and Tarquin had departed in Honor's little ship. Incredibly, however, the destruction had nevertheless occurred.

Chapter 19

Rescue

NEARLY a solar day had passed since the explosion aboard the Wolfen ship. Merlin patiently searched, aware of the lingering looks he increasingly received from Gall, Tarquin, and other crew members. Gall was remarkably cooperative, allowing Merlin to give orders on his bridge. Merlin knew that his father was considering how to persuade him that this search was no longer likely to be successful. Yet, stubbornly, Merlin refused to acknowledge this. He nearly leapt up when Tarquin's calm voice announced, "Approaching yet another group of debris. Several large objects. Scanning now."

"Tarquin?" Merlin asked quickly, his eyes on the screen.

"Several pieces of what appears to have been the starboard nacelle, cylindrical in shape, plus one other object. Eight-sided, approximately four meters across…" Tarquin flashed a glance at his son.

In moments Merlin also saw the object in question. It resembled a large tortoise with magnetic clamp-ended legs. It was octagon-shaped, and appeared to be a maintenance pod of the type used by larger ships for major exterior hull repair in areas where dangerous energy leaks had occurred. They were generally anchored to the outer hull by thick umbilical cables secured near the engineering control areas. This pod was designed to make its way along the outer surface of the hull to reach any problem area. It was also heavily shielded to withstand extended periods of raw radiation while protecting its occupants. Merlin recalled seeing the pod on the shuttle bay deck of the Wolfen ship.

Now he saw that the umbilical had been ripped free. In addition to supplying power and computer access to the mechanisms and sensors aboard the pod, this cable also powered its maneuvering abilities if it was disconnected from its magnetic couplings. The pod tumbled slowly in space, with one of its thick legs torn off. Its power cable floated by its mooring, extended and wrinkled, resembling the discarded skin of a snake. No illumination showed through its eight ports, and the scan indicated that internal atmospheric controls were not functioning.

Gall growled low in his throat and then said, "For just a moment, I thought I detected a short-range com signal from that pod. The type used in space dock between repair crews. It's gone now. It was very weak and contained no message, like a link left open in an empty cabin."

Feeling his heart speed up, Merlin whispered, "Honor!" He stared at the screen, his mind racing. "Do our sensors tell us anything?"

"There's still too much residual interference," was the terse reply. "Each of these is hot with radiation."

Merlin's claws tapped the controls, giving the ship orders to extend a tractor arm and pull the pod closer. "I want to get inside that thing and look around," he said.

"Careful Merlin," Tarquin cautioned. "If you touch that pod with any kind of energy, its exostructure may destabilize. Energy pressure alone may rupture it."

Merlin nodded, his claw tips still hovering over the control boards.

Gall pointed out: "We have telescoping grapplers in the cargo handling area. It may be possible to remove one to the bay doors and then draw the pod inside the ship through the larger opening. Of course, such an accommodation will take time to arrange."

Shaking his head, Merlin said, "If Honor's aboard that pod, time is the one thing she doesn't have. I need to get close enough to get aboard that pod!" He got to his feet now, saying, "I need to get our ship as close as possible, Tarquin. Then I'll use Honor's shuttle to pull up beside it, clamp onto it, and then board the pod wearing an enviro suit."

"Merlin, we don't *know* that Honor is even aboard that pod," Tarquin pointed out.

Gall stepped up beside the elder felinoid, grunting in agreement with him.

Meeting their eyes steadily, Merlin responded, "Don't we?"

Tarquin shrugged slightly, then nervously licked a paw, knowing better than to argue with his strong-willed son. Gall snorted, making a sound of surrender.

Merlin quickly realized that wearing an environmental suit inside Honor's little shuttle made maneuvering more than a little challenging. After managing to clamp onto the slowly-spinning pod, it took a few ticks longer to stabilize it before he could locate an access portal to get inside. Depressurization seemed to take much longer than usual. Finally, Merlin was able to release the seals and open the shuttle's hatch.

Through the comlink in the helmet near his left ear, Merlin heard Tarquin report, "Radiation levels still interfere with determining if there is anyone alive inside the pod. Clearly the Wolfen ship's outer hull had breached first. That blast tore this pod free from its coupling cables and launched it like a projectile, thereby protecting it from the full force of the secondary explosion that would have disintegrated it."

His father's voice was calm and cool as usual, but Merlin could hear the tension behind it. Tarquin was also fond of Honor, and was also very concerned about her survival.

Finally Merlin was able to pop the hatch and push his way over to the work pod, which rocked unsteadily when he attached a towing cable to secure it. The cable pulled taut and then stabilized. Merlin pulled a now-weightless oxygen tank behind himself and, using handholds on the pod, he found the docking port where oxygen was generally fed into the structure. He kept up a running narrative with Tarquin as he worked and finished by reporting that the pod was re-pressurizing as fresh oxygen was pumped into it. Again, it seemed far too long before Merlin read a level indicating that it might be safe to open the pod's outer airlock door. He slipped into the portal, secured the door behind himself, and then manually cranked open the inner airlock.

There was no gravity inside and the only light was that reflected from the nearby larger ship, shining dimly through its ports. Merlin switched on the helmet lamp of his suit and shone it around the small area. Several humanoid bodies floated weightlessly, deflated, as if their bones and flesh had somehow been sucked out of the environmental suits encompassing them. It took Merlin a moment to realize that these were only empty suits, and they had not been occupied. Such equipment was generally secured to the restraint webs upon the walls when not in use. These had been strewn about as if someone had rifled through them, looking for something. Each suit's equipment pack had been torn open and their oxygen processors had been ripped free from them.

Then Merlin saw Honor.

Wearing one of the suits, she hung limply from the restraint webbing secured to an upright pillar. Nine oxygen packs had been hastily linked with common tubing to stretch the air supply of her suit. Her faceplate was smeared with something dark and he could not see her face clearly but from her size he was certain who it was.

"I've found her, Tarquin!" Merlin reported excitedly. Then, snapping a fresh oxygen pack to her suit, he freed and discarded the nearly spent ones. The restraint webbing around her suit had become very tangled, so he produced a utility blade to cut her free.

"What is her condition?" Tarquin's calm voice inquired over the link.

"I can't say yet," Merlin replied. "She seems to be unconscious. I'm coming out with her now."

Easily swinging the woman up in his arms, Merlin flinched when his work light shone directly onto her faceplate. It reflected back red with spattered blood from both inside and outside the suit. Honor's face was turned to the side, but he could still see that she had bled from her ears and nose, and her lips were blue.

Merlin hurried to the shuttle ship, carrying Honor in his arms like a child. Hissing, he said over the voice link: "Tarquin, tell Gall we'll need the medical systems activated. There is bleeding from her ears and nose. I don't know how she's survived this long!"

"The lady is very much like Drakyn, lad," Tarquin responded

evenly. "Very resilient. Is there any sign of him aboard the pod?"

"No one else. Just Honor," Merlin replied.

Four hours later Merlin was dozing, sitting beside Honor's bunk aboard the *Serpentine*. Gall and the medical computers had done most of the immediate work necessary, including transfusing an alarming four units of concentrated human blood and sealing a gaping puncture wound in her shoulder that had cracked her collarbone. A normal human would have died almost immediately from her wounds and the blood loss, but the non-human part of her nature had maintained Honor's life force. Both of Honor's eardrums had been punctured as a result of the Wolfen ship's explosion. However, scans also showed that her body was quickly healing itself, regenerating nerves and mending damaged tissues. She would survive; she would heal.

A soft sound made Merlin's head snap up and turn toward the woman. Her eyes were open, though somewhat glassy and unfocussed. When he moved closer she seemed to focus upon him sharply and she murmured something too softly for him to understand. Merlin took her hand in his big paw and stroked it to convey reassurance. He resisted his feline inclination to lick her skin and instead lowered his head to rub it against the back of her hand.

Her fingers stroked his heavy fur affectionately and then she said slowly and precisely, "Drakyn? The Wolfen? Gone?"

Raising his head, he nodded and replied, "Gone."

"No! Not..!" Honor disagreed, shaking her head and then trying to pull herself up.

Merlin caught her shoulders and easily held her down. "Rest! Stay there!"

Honor slumped against him, whispering, "Where is he? I didn't..."

It took Merlin a moment realize that the med-system had automatically injected Honor with a powerful painkiller and she was already asleep again.

***

HONOR awakened with a ringing in her ears. When she moved, a sharp pain in her shoulder brought her immediately to full consciousness. She blinked up at the overhead lights and then turned her head to squint at the sensor board above the bed. She recognized the sick bay area of the *Serpentine*, and noted that her heart was beating at a reasonable rate. Then she frowned, because she could not hear any of the normal clicks and beeps of the equipment.

Tentatively, she slid a leg over the side of her bed and pulled herself up into a sitting position. Nausea struck her suddenly, so she breathed through her mouth until it passed. Her nose felt sore too, as if she had taken a punch there, but it did not seem to be broken. Gritting her teeth, she made herself stand up and then nearly fell backward as both her ears suddenly cleared with a *pop* that seemed loud enough to shake the ship. At last she could hear the pulsing of the sensor equipment, so she smiled and pulled the bracelet-like leads from her wrist.

By the time Merlin made it back to sick bay, Honor was seated at a computer terminal in the room, bringing up data.

"You're supposed to be resting," he pointed out, pleased in spite of his concern.

"Hush sweetie," she replied calmly, "You're wasting your breath. Anyhow, according to the medical computer I'm supposed to be deaf for another 24 hours or so anyhow. It's wrong, by the way." She turned to grin at him, and then added, "Hey, Gall! Hi, Tarquin!"

The elder felinoid appeared in the doorway with Gall, who rumbled, "Honor, you look much recovered, but…"

His words were cut off when Honor got to her feet and embraced him affectionately, saying, "Thank you for all you've done to help me heal, Gall. You're very talented. However, I feel much better, so don't try to boss me around. In fact, what kind of blood did you guys give me? I'm almost giddy. I think I've had more than enough of it!"

Effortlessly, the big engineer picked Honor up from her feet and set her back upon the diagnostic table, growling, "How do your ears feel? Let me get a few readings here…"

"My ears work fine, thanks. I've run a diagnostic myself and I'm nearly 100% back to what passes for normal for me!"

"I'll decide that myself, Honor," Gall grumbled.

"Yes, yes, oh talented one!" Honor replied in an attempt to sound meek that made even Tarquin's eyes widen.

Merlin sniffed audibly, trying not to show the others how

amused he was watching them. Few people ever had the energy to argue with Gall, and Tarquin was an imposing male felinoid, but Honor knew how to disarm them so easily. Honor made it worse by catching Merlin's eye and remarking, "They are adorable, aren't they, Merlin?"

Thankfully Merlin was spared a reply as Gall growled softly at them all, glared at the readings, and then left the sick bay saying over his shoulder, "She's fit enough..."

"I will return to the bridge," Tarquin said in a dignified tone.

Smiling playfully, Honor said, "Merlin, will you please brief me on what happened? How did you guys get me off the Wolfen ship?"

Merlin sat beside her and rubbed his cheek against hers as he answered, "We didn't, Honor. That ship was destroyed by internal explosions."

"That much I figured. I started the reaction within the ship's systems," she said, as she leaned against him comfortably.

Staying on subject, Merlin went on, "We never saw a shuttle leave the ship, and when the situation became critical we kept our distance as you instructed. I knew you'd find a way out of there. After the ship broke up, we searched for you in every likely piece of the ship, hoping an escape pod would be near it, or attached to it. We found you inside a work pod that had been torn free during the break-up of the ship's outer hull. You were in an enviro suit, held by restraint webbing with nine oxygen packs fed into it. You don't remember doing that?"

Honor looked at him for a long moment, a little frown creasing her forehead. "No." she replied. "The last thing I remember is heading for the shuttle bay to get off the ship. I was wounded, and I remember falling. I must have blacked out. My shoulder hurt when I hit the deck... You say I was alone in the pod?"

"Yes, Honor, you were alone," Merlin replied.

After hesitating for a moment, Honor told Merlin what had occurred aboard the Wolfen ship after he and Tarquin had left. She detailed Krell's physical attack upon Drakyn and what had happened afterward. Sighing, she admitted, "There's so much about Drakyn's nature that I still don't know or understand! I don't know if he's really dead or not. I don't *feel* him like I always could, but I don't accept that he's gone. Maybe it's false hope on my part. Only time will answer that question, I guess. Even so, I don't think I got myself into that work pod. But if that's true, where is he?"

Unable to provide any kind of answer to that question, Merlin remained silent.

Chapter 20

Acceptance

MERLIN found himself watching Honor carefully when she insisted on getting out of sickbay and moving around the ship as if she had never been injured. Certainly part of his watchfulness was directly related to his concern for her health, but another part was his uncertainty about her emotional state. As tough as Honor pretended to be, Merlin nevertheless knew she had been devastated by the disappearance of Drakyn from her life. There had been something very special, beyond the bond of lovers, between the great Lord of Viste and Honor.

Certainly no one else had been able to inflame and then defuse Drakyn's violent moods and furious bouts of temper as Honor could with a few softly murmured words. The two of them were known to have had extremely loud arguments that involved demonstrations of temper from both parties. Merlin had never completely understood, once she had returned to her duties with the Fleet, why Honor had nevertheless willingly returned to Drakyn as if to a safe and familiar harbor. It was difficult for him to even imagine Honor without Drakyn's mostly-silent influence in the atmosphere surrounding her.

Honor had stopped talking about Drakyn, other than the few things she had uttered right after she had been rescued from the oxygen depleted shuttle. So Merlin, Gall, and Tarquin went about the ship's business in silence on the matter. Yet Merlin maintained his own quiet vigil, hoping that Honor would reach for him as her surrogate son when and if she needed his comfort and support.

When Merlin told her that they were taking the ship out of this sector, heading toward Viste, Honor offered no objections—indeed, no comments at all, and such a lack of opinion worried him.

As soon as she could, Honor went down to the shuttle bay and inspected the *Freedom*. The shuttle required a few minor repairs, and Merlin suggested that he and Gall could assist with the work.

He was almost relieved when she disagreed, saying, "No, I need to do this."

So she undertook doing the work alone, laboring for a solar week with the sort of unflagging, obsessive energy that she had always demonstrated. Eventually she took the ship out and tested it for more than twenty hours, and returned pronouncing that she was satisfied with the results.

During the next morning watch, Honor came to Merlin at the post he had assumed on the bridge. Gall was elsewhere, so they were alone when she announced to Merlin that she had something to tell him.

Before he could reply, she stated, "It's time for me to go..."

Merlin's prehensile tail wrapped itself around his forepaw so tightly that the paw went numb. Deliberately, he relaxed his muscles and the appendage released its nervous grip. Taking a hissing breath, the handsome felinoid whispered, "Explain to me what you mean, Honor. Please."

"I'm leaving," Honor replied readily enough, meeting his gaze evenly. Her eyes were calm and clear. "I've contacted Admiral Kimitake at Fleet headquarters and I've resigned my position, effective immediately. It's time for me to move on, and to find a new path. I need to change my life now."

"You truly want to break away from the Fleet?" he asked. "I can understand, I suppose, after all the years you've served. But what about Port Viste? It's still your home, Honor. Will you go there? Pried and the others need to be told what's occurred and why Drakyn won't be returning. Viste has been ruled by Drakyn for so long!" Even as he asked the question, Merlin knew he was sounding like a nervous adolescent.

Honor flashed one of her sweet human smiles and put her small hand over his giant paw, smoothing the fur with two fingers just as she had done when he was a kitten growing up on planet Viste. "You're taking Tarquin home, aren't you? Viste is *your* home, love. Not mine, despite the fact that I lived there for some years. Without Drakyn, I can't even consider going back..."

Her voice broke and she cleared her throat softly before adding, "Tarquin and Pried ker D'at will know what to do now. Don't worry, pussycat. Viste will be there for you, when and if you're done serving with the Fleet as well. I've transferred ownership of the *Serpentine* to Gall now."

"It isn't that, Honor!" Merlin murmured, arching his whiskers in concern. "I just have the terrible feeling that we're...that you and I are saying a final farewell. Don't run away from the people who love you. We all do, you know!"

Shaking her head, Honor smiled and replied, "One never knows when or if a final farewell is being spoken, sweetie. You know that I care about you and that I would never willingly or knowingly abandon you forever, Merlin. We have a wonderful and significant history together, don't we? But, perhaps this time I will be away longer than in the past. Believe me, there's nothing to be concerned about. Remember, I don't age like other...like humans do. We'll see each other again."

"You may not age, but I do!" Merlin replied sorrowfully.

"You will always be a kitten to me, Merlin," she replied warmly. "Hug now?"

The giant felinoid gladly engulfed Honor's little form between his arms in an embrace. Honor happily buried her face in his thick fur, rubbing the side of her face against him until he leaned over and did the same against her face. Suddenly he uttered an involuntary purring sound that made Honor and then him laugh aloud in surprise. Purring was a kitten sound he had abandoned with adolescent posturing, and Honor had always teased him about missing it.

"I love you, sweetie," Honor said gently, but clearly. "Now, let me go so I can fly my ship. I'll contact you whenever I can through Fleet channels, or other channels on Viste, or wherever I find you."

Merlin inclined his head, not trusting his own voice.

Flashing her grin at him again, Honor turned and walked through the sliding doors into the curving corridor that led to the shuttle bay.

As he watched her go, Merlin silently noted that her shadow wavered upon the curved wall behind her as she walked, and for just a moment there was an optical illusion—but it was quickly gone. For a heartbeat of time, Merlin imagined he saw a second shadow moving at Honor's side, tall and strong, with a cape falling like wings from muscular male shoulders.

Blinking, Merlin looked again and saw only Honor moving out of sight.

Yet, for some reason, Merlin felt comforted.

Within twenty ticks, Merlin, Tarquin, and Gall were all together again on the bridge observing the departure of the small shuttle known as the *Freedom*. The sleek little ship moved free of the ship's shuttle bay, did a farewell roll and then slipped quickly away from visual contact. At the proper distance from the larger ship, the *Freedom's* star drive was engaged, and in a flash of energy she disappeared from their tracking screens.

Chapter 21

Everything...

WHAT drove my decision to break away from Fleet service, I cannot truly put into words in this record. It felt necessary, rather like a priority after losing Drakyn. I felt bereft and I assumed it was grief, as I mourned the most powerful, life-changing love I might ever experience. A long life without him seemed impossible to me.

After departing from the *Serpentine*, my intention was to return to Earth for a short time to wrap up my business dealings there. The time I had been in service to the Fleet was well beyond my contractual commitment. Although Admiral Kimitake was not pleased when I reached him on a link, he knew he could not dissuade me from this decision. He was aware, as well as I, that I had been living on borrowed luck for years, and our agreement had always been that I was free to resign my work at any time, as I was no longer officially part of the military.

It would take more than two weeks to travel back to Earth in my little ship, but I was happy for the solitude to do some serious thinking about what my next step might be. I still owned property on Earth that had come to me from my long-deceased family, but the idea of living there did not appeal to me at all. Managers took care of the property without my direct involvement, and had I arranged years ago for Merlin to have access to any income it generated.

Strangely, I did not feel that I should mourn Drakyn. I felt emotionally silent, even comforted in a strange way. On some level I was certain that our parting was only temporary, despite the evidence I had witnessed. Drakyn was still with me, and would remain close to me for however long I lived. I did know that I had inherited so many of his powers, so much of his skills and abilities, that I was probably more powerful and resilient than most living humanoids, and a large number of non-humanoid entities. This was Drakyn's gift to me.

With my ship's course set and locked, I was free to sit and enjoy the enormity of the universe as it spread out before my tiny vessel. My options were myriad, and my power was all Drakyn's.

He had repeated often that we were joined in spirit and mind, and that all I needed to do was call out and he would hear and respond to my summons. Was it possible, even when the laws of the universe assured me that I had witnessed Drakyn's death, that I might have been wrong? I pondered this thought, feeling my heart rate increase in excitement and hope until it felt as if it might burst from my chest.

So, after preparing my ship for the voyage, I composed myself and reached inward. Imagine my surprise when almost at once a shout sounded in my brain, a call for attention and a demand for release. Immediately, I recognized the tone of the command, the lack of patience, and the arrogant assurance as none other than Drakyn—my lover-protector-mentor, dear monster, and occasional hero. I had seen him pierced to the heart and watched his body turn to vapor while I held him in my arms, and I believed that he was lost to me.

The moment I recognized his consciousness, I willingly offered Drakyn anything he would need to help him return to human form, to this plane of existence.

"Open your eyes," I heard him command.

Obeying him, I found Drakyn standing before me. He was the same large and handsome humanoid I knew so well, but he had somehow aged many, many years. Despite his admitted very long life, his appearance had always been that of a tall, black-haired and powerful humanoid in the prime of life. Now his black hair was completely white and fell halfway down his back, and his face was lined with years. However, his dark blue eyes burned as fiercely as the day we had first encountered each other.

Murmuring his name in relief, I reached out to him, wanting the touch to confirm his reality. His abrupt gesture halted me.

"*No*," he hissed, his voice rasping like a very old man. "You imperil yourself seriously if you touch me now, Honor! This form is very difficult to hold, and your proximity puts even more pressure on me. I might kill you if we touched now."

Staring at him, it physically hurt me to withdraw my arms and just look at him. "Drakyn, you have never, and could never, hurt me!"

"Woman!" he snarled, his extended teeth visible, "I am not myself! Do not test me on this!"

Blinking at his ferocity, I relaxed back onto my seat saying softly, "You've shown yourself here for a reason. You know I'll do whatever you ask of me to help you." Involuntary tears came to my eyes as I added, "I really didn't know what I'd do without you..."

"Stop. I have no way to comfort you, Honor. You have just offered me your assistance, but I must be fair with you and warn you that if you truly commit to the steps I am here to propose, there can be no turning back from the path you will take. It will not be an easy path, little one, and your own life, health, and even possibly your sanity shall be put at risk. You enjoy your existence as it is now, do you not? The particular strengths you gained from me will become almost irrelevant in this effort, and you are likely to find yourself struggling even to survive!"

"Drakyn," I said calmly, "I would not have survived this long without you. How can I do less than help you?"

Drakyn shook his head, closed his eyes for a moment as if to gather his strength before saying, "Again, I caution you that if you come with me, circumstances will be extremely different. When we next meet, I surely will not even recognize you. It is likely that I could be the cause of great torment to you, possibly even your murder. I do not wish to cause you pain, Honor, nor do I wish to be the tool of your destruction."

"Hush, you would not..!" I began.

"Wait!" He raised a hand, fixing those dark eyes firmly upon mine in a manner that chilled me. "This involves returning to where I began, to my past and my racial family. Among some of my kind, you will seem little more than meat to starving beasts! Imagine an entire race of beings like me in nature—warriors, prone to violence and natural blood drinkers. You alone will be responsible for protecting yourself among them, and I will be a danger to you rather than a protector! There will also be new and terrible enemies for you to battle, in addition to me. Please understand this before you make a decision!"

There was a long moment of silence between us as I stared at him, considering what he said. I knew he was serious. I should be afraid, and yet I was not. This was still the being I had learned to love years ago, the man who had taught me incredible things, and who always cherished me, despite his solitary mannerisms. I was more like him than my birth race now. I would never be content to remain among humans or even the mix of people who occupied Viste.

At last, I asked him, "Drakyn, do you trust that I will do everything possible to succeed among your people?"

His face showed pain I had never seen there before as he admitted, "I have never known anyone I trust as much as you, Honor."

"You know I will come with you," I declared, "but you must promise me something here and now. It must be a vow." Heedless of his earlier warning, I put a light hand upon his arm, not withdrawing it even when he again showed his blood teeth.

"What is the promise?" he snarled unhappily.

"You have always claimed you were incapable of love," I reminded him gently. "I don't believe that, but I won't argue with you. What I want from you is the promise to remember forever my love for *you*, and to allow your own heart to be guided by it."

"Honor, I am certain that I shall lose any memory of you!" he protested.

"Maybe," I replied. "That will be difficult for me, but I believe your heart will remember me on some level, however deeply buried. I truly believe this. Do you trust that I know more about love than you do?"

My arrogant self-assurance came from somewhere within me that could not be denied. I understood that I truly did hold the next portion of my life in my hands and whatever I willed to be so, could be made to happen. In retrospect, I recalled the old saying about being careful what you wish for.

Drakyn nodded slowly, as I knew he would. He whispered, "I do promise you, Honor. Somehow, somewhere at the very root of my being, I shall remember you, honor you, and be guided by the love you bear in your incredibly generous heart. Now that you've made your decision, I can assure you that despite whatever challenges and pain you suffer moving forward, there will also be great adventures, pleasure, and unforgettable love. Many reasons for joy..."

"I love you, Drakyn," I said. "Now, tell me what is to be done."

He extended a hand to me and I took it without hesitation.

Moving slowly, he raised my hand to his mouth for a moment before he replied, "We must return to where and *when* I originated. My energies are weak right now, so your personal life energy is necessary to hold us together and guide us through this passage of time and space. I will be destroyed and re-formed as I once was. Return to this time and place may be impossible for us, little one. Now, for all I might ever do or cause to happen to you, please forgive me, Honor."

Aware of the trembling of his now-fragile hand, I tightened my hold upon it. "Let's go," I said.

His so-dark eyes met and held mine. "An anomaly is forming outside this ship. Disengage the deflectors now and allow it to take us inside. Try not to feel fear..."

My ship's sensors confirmed his words and I stared at what appeared to be some kind of black hole revealing itself. Drawing a deep and steadying breath, I reached over the navigation console and did the unthinkable, the suicidal. I released the helm controls.

In an instant the universe turned inside out. It was as if the space around my tiny ship had somehow developed a sentient mind, and it broke inside the ship. Time seemed slowed to a crawl and yet sped by intolerably in the same instant. Nothing and everything made any sense to me. I heard voices laughing and shouting, screams and wails, a strangely breathy singing and the echoing cry of an infant. I watched Drakyn's aged body dissolving again into vapor and dispersing itself around the cabin in a miniature whirlwind that grew in intensity until the screaming air deafened me. It took all of my strength to grab onto and hold myself against the pilot seat, but after a while even that strength failed me. I felt as if I was at the mouth of an enormous vacuum tube that pulled at me irresistibly as my hands grew numb.

I was dragged inexorably astern, grasping desperately at the floor grids but unable to secure any handhold. Looking back over my shoulder I saw a huge black void where my ship's aft compartments should have been. The rushing air was cold and dark, yet it was not an airless void of space. A strange song filled my mind.

This was some kind of dimensional time shift, I decided, as the empty, black mouth sucked me inside and into a kind of dim, dreamless and comfortless interval between unconsciousness and death. Through this, the breathy singing voice comforted me somehow and I mentally cherished it as a beacon, as an anchor of hope for the future.

LaVergne, TN USA
10 November 2010
204313LV00004B/77/P